ALL HARTS AND FLOWERS

KELLY BRIGHT

All Harts and Flowers is a work of fiction. Any references to historical events, real people, or real places are used fictitiously. Other names, characters, places, and events are products of the author's imagination, and any resemblance to actual events or places or persons, living or dead, is entirely coincidental.

2023 Standards of Starlight Paperback Edition

www.standardsofstarlight.com

ISBN: 978-1-952893-19-3

Cover art by Elizabeth Mackey

A NOTE FROM THE AUTHOR

KELLY BRIGHT

Wondering where The Romantics series is set?

Welcome to the fictional Southern town of Loveland, Tennessee, located just southwest of Nashville!

Loveland is based on the real town of Franklin, Tennessee.

In my novels, Loveland is west of downtown Franklin in a mostly rural area between there and Fairview. In real life, that stretch includes a quaint little village called Lieper's Fork which is popular with the country music crowd. I've sort of expanded on the Village of Lieper's Fork and made Loveland a twin town to Franklin, if you will.

I lived and owned 2.2 acres there until recently, when I moved east within the Nashville metro area to be closer to a university Mr. Bright and the Bright Boys are attending.

In my novels, I've included many of my favorite places—the Natchez Trace Parkway Bridge, Puckett's Grocery, and Loveless Cafe, to name a few—plus added new, fictional spots to bring the stories to life.

I hope you enjoy reading all about it.

—Kelly

CHAPTER 1

ROSALIE

"Act natural," the cameraman says, as if it's the easiest thing in the world.

Sure. Okay. Not.

I smile broadly and drop my shoulders to what I hope is a natural-looking position. "How's this?" I ask. I can feel that my neck is now angled funny, and my hands are balled into tight fists.

"Better," he says, "but I'd love to see you even more at ease, Ms. Flowers. Pretend we aren't here."

I laugh nervously, my eyes widening as I try to imagine how I'm going to survive ten months of this. Ten months! I am, apparently, not great in front of a camera.

In my defense, there's a clunky wireless microphone tucked into the waistband of my skirt. It's positioned on my back, but it's pulling the material tight against the front and making me feel self conscious about my belly. Not to mention, no less than three people are following me around with various pieces of equipment. One guy even smells. *Yuck.* Judging by the sheen on his hair, I don't think he's fond of bathing. I catch an unpleasant whiff every time he hoists the boom pole in my direction.

Hey, at least I'm learning video production terminology. I feel fancy tossing around terms like boom pole.

"Get it together," my friend and business partner, Ella Lovelace, says in a low growl as she elbows me. "Don't ruin this for us, Rosie."

"I won't," I mutter. "Trust me. That's the last thing I want to do."

Landing this show was a huge break. Not just for my flower shop and me, personally, but for my two besties. The three of us co-own the wedding services group together. Within the larger collaborative, Clara Darling owns a travel agency that caters to the wedding industry and Ella owns a bridal boutique.

I know, I know. Rosalie Flowers, the woman who owns a flower shop and whose best friends also have sugary-sweet last names. It's almost too much. Just go with it. We've made it work.

Ella's grandpa started calling us The Romantics at one point when we were kids, and the nickname stuck. Everyone knows our trio as such. We even use it as the official name for the group of wedding-industry businesses we head up. It's out there on the front of the building in big, silver letters next to the gooseneck lanterns: *The Romantics.*

Once this character-driven documentary series is produced by the good folks at our local public broadcasting network, the name will be known far and wide. *Our* names will be known far and wide.

Yikes.

I narrow my eyes, wondering what the series will be called. I could probably offer a few suggestions. *Romancing in a Small Southern Town?* Accurate, but nah, too clunky. *Romancing the Bride?* That one's better, but it isn't quite right. Sometimes we have two brides, or two grooms. Hmm … Something about rose-colored glasses, maybe, as a play on my name? Assuming, of course, that I'm the star.

I *am* the leader of our threesome. Sort of.

Wait, though. Did that sound sexual? It did. I'm getting ahead of myself.

"Rosie will be okay," Clara says warmly, drawing my attention back to the present moment.

I clear my throat, then gesture in the air as I talk. "Um, yeah, I will definitely be okay. I'll get acclimated to this. My mama always used to say that I'm nothing if not adaptable. The only constant in life is change, right?"

The cameraman flashes a knowing smile. "Sure thing," he says.

He doesn't ask about the past tense I used for my mama. We don't know each other well enough for personal questions just yet.

Oh, well. He's probably accustomed to people like me who aren't comfortable in the spotlight. He'll probably have a good laugh at my expense the moment I'm out of his ear shot.

I don't care. I'm sure I'm funny. Or that I look

funny. Like a clumsy creature of some sort. An egret that isn't too good at landings, maybe. All legs and wings flapping about unceremoniously. I saw such a bird on a ferry ride once. No idea why it's coming to mind now.

Wow, that was oddly specific.

At any rate, I hear that this production team worked on a show about a chef and her husband in Eastern North Carolina and another one about a husband-wife singing duo and their farm. That one was based somewhere else in the Carolinas. I forget exactly where. It doesn't matter much. The point is—none of the stars of those shows were used to being filmed when they started, but they made it through the process, somehow.

"Say," I muse, extending my hand for the camera guy to shake, "Welcome to small-town Loveland, Tennessee. I'm Rosalie Flowers."

"I know who you are," he replies with a chuckle. He takes my hand.

The man is old enough to be my dad, and he has a fatherly vibe about him. His short silver hair cropped close against his head reminds me of a military officer in a movie. I wonder if he's ever found himself on the other side of the lens.

"Right, right," I say. "Of course, you know who I am. You're the cameraman. Duh. Please tell me your name again?"

"I'm Sonny Hoover. Nice to meet you," he says. He glances down at the floor sheepishly, then up again. "Although, we've already met. I told you my name when

I walked in the door this morning. Have you forgotten already?"

With this, Ella elbows me again, harder this time. I'm officially embarrassing her. "You remember. Mr. Hoover is not just a cameraman," she whispers urgently. "He's a *producer*. It was all in the email. Did you read the email? What's wrong with you today?"

I shake my head to clear it. "I'm so sorry," I say. "Where are my manners? Yes, Mr. Hoover, It's nice to meet you, too. I'm a fan of your work. That show about the chef and her husband was very well done."

"You watched?" he asks, perking up.

I haven't seen it and can't lie. "Well, not exactly, but I saw the trailer. Friends have told me that every single episode is good."

His shoulders droop, ever so slightly, and he shoves a hand in his pants pocket. "Oh. Okay."

"I've seen all five seasons," Clara announces triumphantly, jumping in and taking the pressure off of me. She pushes a section of her long brown hair over one shoulder then raises her arm in the air like the teacher's pet we all know she is. "The series is fabulous. Top notch. The scenery on the farm and at the restaurant is simply gorgeous. Watching it on screen makes me want to go visit North Carolina and taste the food for myself. I suppose that was the goal, wasn't it? If so, I'd say you did well for those folks. Kudos, Mr. Hoover."

Sonny basks in the compliment, his bushy brows parting as he smiles. "I'm glad to hear that, Ms. Darling. It's always nice to meet a fan." He adjusts his belt absentmindedly and leans back, like he might make a speech. "You just wait. Once your show is ready, fans will be approaching you to say how much they liked you on screen. All three of you. They'll want to come to Tennessee and hire you ladies to assist with their weddings."

Ella steps forward, acting as a confident spokesperson for our group. "We trust that will happen," she says with a genuine smile. Then, after a pause, "give us a few minutes, would you, sir? Clara and I will make sure Rosalie here has her game face on by the time you return."

"Probably a good idea," I mumble.

Sonny lowers his brow and nods. "Take as long as you need. I could use a smoke." He must notice the look of revulsion on my face because he appears ashamed. "It's a disgusting habit, I know. Wish I could quit. Maybe someday."

Ella, Clara and I assure him it's no big deal—even though it kind of is—then we excuse ourselves and make our way to a lounge area near the door to my shop. Sonny motions to the production crew members, who put their equipment down and scatter.

Within a few short minutes, the three of us are alone. All except for a young woman manning a mobile coffee kiosk near the exterior door.

She's new. We inked the deal with the local coffee brewing company last week. They'll sell coffee right here in our building during limited hours. Hopefully, it will be a win-win. Our clients will have access to tasty, locally-made beverages, and the brewing company can pick up a bit of new business.

I'll introduce myself to her soon enough. It looks like she needs time to get her display right before she can open for the day, anyway. She's whirling around, stacking paper cups and stirring canisters of hot liquid.

I plop down on a leather easy chair, my limbs piled haphazardly around me.

We're in the lobby area of the building. Sonny wanted to start filming here, for obvious reasons. My friends and I were intentional about keeping a minimalist style in the space, but it suddenly feels like it's too sparse. Nothing seems quite right.

I feel off kilter for some reason. Maybe it's just nerves getting the better of me. Like my mama used to say, I need to take a chill pill.

"Ugh," I groan as I settle deeper into the chair.

"What?" Ella asks.

"This is exhausting," I say. "Not to look the gift horse in the mouth or anything."

"Are you calling Sonny a horse?" Clara asks.

I smirk. The humor coursing below the surface feels familiar. And good.

My assistant, Rachael Drye, is at the counter in my shop. She can see us through the wall of glass, but can't hear us. I glance over and give her a smile, then a thumbs up. She's eagerly waiting for her turn on camera.

This is a big, momentous day for everyone involved.

Ella sits beside me, but she maintains a formal posture. She probably doesn't want to wrinkle her carefully tailored dress. "Rosie," she says, "we need to get you laid. You're too high strung."

Clara has taken a sip of diet soda, and she nearly spits it all over the floor. "Ella!" she exclaims. She's standing, at least, so any spittage will stay clear of our leather chairs.

I roll my eyes. I don't think the coffee lady can hear our conversation. She doesn't react. *Thank God.*

"Am I wrong?" Ella asks without a trace of embarrassment in her expression.

Clara scoffs. "I don't know, but have a little couth. Would you? A little class? Just a smidge."

Ella shrugs. "I speak the truth. You know that. Rosie's in a funk. She acts like she has a stick up her ass. If we could arrange for a stick up her lady lane, she might relax long enough to get this filming underway."

"Lady lane?" I ask with a laugh. "That's a new one."

Clara giggles, a smile spreading across her face. For someone as straight laced as she is, she sure does enough giggling at our risque references.

"You knew what I meant, didn't you?" Ella replies. "And I'm serious. It's been too long, Rosie. You need *serviced*, if you get my drift."

I scowl. "How do you know how long it's been? Huh? Do you have a hidden camera outside my bedroom door?"

"No," Ella says, wagging a finger playfully, "but that isn't a bad idea. I could probably have one installed by the time you arrive home this evening."

"Why don't you bug her phone or something?" Clara asks, joining in the fun. "Might as well go all the way."

"Umm hmm," Ella parrots. *"All the way."*

We laugh. Barely a second goes by before they continue razzing me.

"Ohhh, I know!" Clara continues. "We could set Rosie up with one of the film crew. The tall redhead is cute."

I reach over and smack my friend on the arm. "Okay, enough already. I hear you both. Loud and clear. But I'm not sleeping with anyone on the film crew. That's asking for trouble."

"*Do you* hear us?" Ella replies.

"I do. Lady lane, stick, etcetera."

Our chit-chat is helping me to loosen up. Sonny will be glad. I'm sure he and his crew would like to get back to business.

"Speaking of lady lanes," I say, "I actually have a date next weekend."

Clara's eyes get big. "You do?" she asks.

"Well, now," Ella says. "Good girl."

I smile, then clear my throat. "I know you want all of the details, but there isn't much to tell yet."

"What does he look like?" Clara asks.

I hunch over, my body language likely to betray my secret. I smooth my skirt. "Not now. Not here," I say. "I'll fill you in when we have more time. I promise."

They nod, but Ella isn't buying it.

"What's wrong?" Clara asks her, noticing the suspicious look on our friend's face. "Ella, do you know who Rosie's date is with?"

Ella shakes her head.

"Then what is it? I know that look," Clara insists. "Ella? *What?*"

I shrug playfully.

"There's no date," Ella says. "Unless it's with an imaginary friend. Or a cousin, or something like that. She's pulling our leg."

"A cousin?!" I ask, pretending to be insulted.

"We *are* in Tennessee," Ella jokes.

"Hey, Ella, you grew up here like the rest of us," I reply. "Just because your family is from New York doesn't mean you can make kissing cousin jokes at our expense. You're a Tennessean, too, through and through. Besides, I've never known any actual kissing cousins around here. We're close enough to Nashville to be more … refined."

Ella sticks her tongue out at me. "Maybe you're right. Seriously, though, don't try to change the subject, Rosie," she says. "There's no date. Zip. Zilch. Nada."

I play coy while Clara acts shocked. I'm not sure if she's actually shocked or if she's finally joining in on our little charade.

After a dramatic pause, I fess up. "Okay, fine," I say. "I don't have a date."

Ella scoffs and rolls her eyes. "See?"

"But I could get one," I add.

"Rosie!" Clara exclaims. "Stop playing."

"I had to do something to get you two vultures off my back," I say, raising my brows while kicking one foot absentmindedly. "At least, I fessed up. I could have told you my date was a well-endowed fellow who pleases me most when he gets wound up … with batteries, that is."

Clara blushes, and her cheeks look like they've been in a winter wind. Only, it's May and pleasantly warm.

"Uh, that's well and good," Ella says. "I'm all for a little—okay, or a lot of—self love, if you know what I mean."

"We know what you mean," I reply. "We always know what you mean."

Ella raises a hand in the air like she's going to snap her fingers. "Rosie, my dear, your pleasure petals need to be kissed by a living, breathing man. One whose touch can drive you wilder than any roboman ever can. One who can treat your lady lane to the most exquisite bump and grind on this side of the Mason-Dixon line."

"Sell it, why don't you?" I ask with a smile.

Ella relaxes her hand and points a finger in my direction. "Tell me, is your sexy slide feeling moist?"

"Okay, enough," Clara says. "Can we not use the word moist? Please? Ugh." She shudders.

"What?" Ella asks. "Moist is … well, moist? It's a nice feeling. Isn't it, Rosie?"

I shrug, playfully. "Maybe." She's right. It's nice, and I'm feeling it. *Moist.* "My love ladder could certainly stand to be climbed."

Ella bounds into the air and pumps a fist. Her enthusiasm is as infectious as an NFL cheerleader's at the Super Bowl. "Look at you!" she exclaims. "Love ladder is a *superb* name for your vag. Aww, Rosie. You're makin' me proud."

"I'm glad," I say, only half joking.

I've never tried to come up with crazy anatomy names like Ella. I'm glad my first effort was well received. It's kind of fun, to be completely honest.

Ella puts an arm around my shoulders. Clara reaches out to squeeze my hand.

We laugh and talk for a while, the tension leaving my body as I enjoy the company of true friends.

If only I knew what the week still held, and how much my life was about to change.

CHAPTER 2

ROSALIE

I'm still draped over the leather chair like it's a lazy summer day on mama's porch when a group of people walk into the lobby, their attention focused on the young woman and the coffee stand.

I don't think these folks are part of the film crew. They must be here to patronize one of our businesses.

"We have company," I say. "Anyone expecting guests?"

Clara and Ella shake their heads.

"Huh," I say. "If not for us, then who?"

We have a couple of temporary tenants in the building, but no other permanent wedding service professionals yet. We intend to bring some more key business owners into the group as soon as possible. The more, the merrier, as far as I'm concerned. I aim for us to become a one-stop shop for our clients.

"Your guess is as good as mine," Clara replies. "But it's a free country. They can do whatever they want."

"In our building?" I ask. "I'm not so sure the free country thing applies."

"It isn't our building yet. Not until the closing next month. I'll say, though, they don't look like they're here for the tattoo guy," she adds.

She's right about that much. Unless the uninitiated have come together for a rip-roaring, wild time this morning, I don't imagine Ledger, the tattoo guy, is getting their business. They don't seem like tattoo types.

"Ledger is his name, Clara," I explain. "Ledger Batson. He's a nice guy. You should get to know him."

"Why? He's only here temporarily."

I shrug. "He might stay on. I don't know."

Clara squirms, as if something has just crawled up the back of her neck. "I'm sure he is a nice enough guy, but is a tattoo parlor the right fit for The Romantics? What do tattoos have to do with weddings, anyway?"

Ella scoffs. "You're a trip, Clara," she says. "Have you been living under a rock for the better part of … I don't know, your life?"

Clara stiffens. "Why would you ask me that?"

"Tell her," I say when Ella eyes me.

Immediately agreeing, Ella slides one slender arm out of her dress. She turns her back to us and looks over her shoulder. As she does, a tiny tattoo in the unmistakable shape of an anchor is revealed. It sits just below her shoulder blade. I've heard the story. Apparently I was right, and Clara isn't in the know.

Clara's eyes grow wide, but she gets her facial expression under control before her jaw actually hits the floor. "Wait," she says. "You have a tattoo? I mean, I see that you have a tattoo. What I want to ask is … Was there a matching version? A couple's tattoo? Who … ?"

The little tattoo is cute. It disappears as quickly as it emerged. I've seen it before, but it's been a long time.

"Yeah, so?" Ella asks as she quickly returns her arm and straightens her dress.

"How did you keep it from me?" Clara asks. "Er, *why* did you keep it from me? I thought we told each other everything."

Now it's my turn to widen my eyes. The fact is, Clara is too uptight in certain situations. Ella and I want to share everything with her, but … well, I suppose I should speak for myself. *I* want to share everything with her, but some details are too racy. Too salacious. Too … morally ambiguous. Or sometimes, just too painful. Clara isn't always the girl you go to for comfort because you might find yourself getting a lecture instead. Sure, Ella is tough as nails and she tells you like it is, but she isn't judgmental like Clara.

Our relationship dynamics are complicated.

"Almost everything," Ella snaps, and we can tell she doesn't intend to talk about it right now.

I decide to stay out of this potential scuffle. To let it burn out before it ignites.

I look away, eager for something or someone to change the subject. Our friend trio is great when things are peaceful, but it can get dicey when sides shift to two against one. We try not to let that happen.

A lean, handsome man in a neat checkered shirt catches my eye.

"Oh, hmm," I say out loud without meaning to.

Maybe I'm moaning because my panties are still wet, like it or not.

I part my lips and raise a finger to them.

The man is with three women of varying ages, but they don't seem to be *with* him. Not in that way. They're probably colleagues. He's tall, with luscious dark hair that fans effortlessly across his strong forehead. When he looks at me, my pulse quickens.

The conversation about pleasure petals and love ladders has me all hot and bothered. Does that put me in a precarious position when spotting a hot hunk of man right in front of me?

Maybe.

Is that a bad thing?

Maybe. Maybe not.

Ella leans over and whispers simply, "go get you some."

I jump, caught off guard. I didn't realize she was noticing me, noticing him. Or him noticing me. Or whatever. I clear my throat. "Uh hmm," I say. "I don't know what you're talking about."

Clara giggles. "Yes, you do. That guy's looking at you."

"Is he?" I ask, sitting up straighter in my chair.

I see him looking at me. Although, Ella or Clara could be the object of his interest, for all I know. They're beautiful ladies. Both are dressed to the nines for filming today. Both could capture any man's heart, if they set their mind to it. Not to mention, Ella just had one entire silky, toned arm splayed out for all to see.

As if on cue, Ella stands. Clara follows her lead, and

the two of them take a few steps away from where I'm sitting. They launch a new, private conversation. Something about the redheaded camera dude Clara mentioned a few minutes ago.

Okay, now I'll admit it. The guy at the coffee stand is definitely looking at me. He's looking *only* at me. I blush, heat warming my cheeks.

He's attractive, that's for sure. Tall, the way I like. Physically fit, too. It appears that he works out.

I'm something of a fitness enthusiast, and I'd love a man who could keep up with me when we inevitably hike the local trails together.

Hiking up to the overlook in Timberland Park above the Natchez Trace Parkway Bridge is, hands down, my favorite Sunday afternoon activity. Insert a hot man and maybe a cute puppy, and I don't think I could find anything better in this big, wide world.

I wouldn't mind seeing this hottie's chiseled features a little closer. I should go and talk to him.

I'm out of practice. "What do I do?" I ask no one in particular.

"Go and talk to him," Ella says, stopping her and Clara's conversation long enough to coach me through this. "If you can work it in, tell him your dick tickler hasn't seen enough action lately."

To that, I laugh out loud. "My dick tickler? Why are these names sounding more and more vulgar? Reign it in, Lovelace."

Ella nods, then raises a smart finger. "You know, your lady lane and—"

"I get it," I say, before she proceeds too far down that ... *lane.*

She is, apparently, a walking thesaurus when it comes to describing women's anatomy in unconventional terms. I should be writing all this down.

I sigh, then look back at the man who now has a steaming beverage in his hand. The ladies with him are smiling and chattering away, while he stares shamelessly in my direction.

This is my chance. I should definitely go and talk to him.

It can't be that hard, right? I can make smalltalk as well as the next gal. It's long past time for me to get back on the horse, er ... the man. To ride again ... er, not ride, like that. Although, maybe like that, too. I sound like Ella.

You know what I mean.

"Rosie," Ella says as she stuffs a twenty into my hand, "go get me a cuppa, would you?"

I spring into action. "Sure, no worries," I reply, standing. Here goes nothing. "Clara, do you want a cuppa?"

"If they have it, I'll take a small chai tea, please," she says sweetly.

"I want mine—" Ella begins, but I cut her off.

"I know, I know," I say. "Black coffee. No cream. Two packs of sugar."

They appear pleased. "What?" I ask rhetorically. "It's almost like we've known each other since we were kids. Relax. And try not to stare like buffoons, please. I'd appreciate a little privacy while I do this."

Clara laughs and nods her agreement, then Ella turns her attention to her phone. I catch a glimpse of the familiar blue and white background on her favorite social site, and I know she'll be occupied for a while. At least, she'll pretend to be occupied. Good enough.

Cash in hand, I walk as nonchalantly as possible toward the coffee stand. I smile at the guy politely as I approach, but I don't want to appear overeager. Instead, I strategically focus on the young woman selling the joe. I'm not good at flirting, so I don't even try. Smalltalk will have to be the extent of it.

Maybe I'll flirt later. Maybe I'll *learn* to flirt later.

I have to consciously tell myself to stop the rambling inner dialogue and focus. I'm not sure my runaway train of thoughts is helpful. Entertaining maybe, but not necessarily helpful.

It gets worse when I'm nervous.

I've always been like that. In my head, I'm a real Chatty Cathy. At least, mama used to call me that. I'm not completely sure what it means.

Focus.

"Good morning. What can I getcha?" the coffee attendant asks. Her name tag reads "Hope." That's an appropriate name for this situation, I suppose.

I *hope* I don't trip over my own feet and embarrass myself. I *hope* I don't spill coffee all over the place and scald anyone. I *hope* this guy is charming. I *hope* Sonny and the film crew stay outside smoking long enough for me to make a connection without it being filmed. I *hope* this guy likes me well enough to give me his number.

"Hi, Hope," I say, then I rattle off our orders.

"Will you need a drink carrier?" she asks when I'm finished.

"Good question," I reply. "My friends are right over there." I turn and glance their way, but as instructed, they don't make eye contact.

"I'll help you carry the cups over to your friends," the handsome guy offers.

Now I have to face him. There's no avoiding it.

Shit.

"That's mighty kind of you," I say with a weird side eye as Hope dutifully pours. It's like I'm looking at him and not, all at the same time. "You don't mind?"

He shrugs, and I must admit that I like the way his shoulder muscles ripple. "Not in the slightest," he says.

"Okay, then," I reply. "I'll take you up on that offer."

I give the cash to Hope, then stand with my hands clenched in front of me as I wait. I probably look like a dork. I probably *am* a dork.

The man seems nervous—or dorky—too, and we continue to eye each other awkwardly while something or another on the coffee cart makes a whizzing sound.

"I'm Jay—" he begins.

At least, I think that's what he says.

Sonny and his crew re-enter the lobby and their loud conversations add to a cacophony of noise that bounces around the space.

I had better hurry this meet cute along.

Is that what this is? Maybe I've read too many romance novels.

I smile and nod at Jay without introducing myself. He probably wouldn't be able to hear me, anyway.

"Almost done," Hope says cheerfully. I think she gets the idea that there's chemistry between Jay and me. She nods and smiles in our direction.

When the beverages are ready, Jay and I grab them.

"Thanks," I say to Hope. "It's great to have you here. In the building, I mean. I hope business is good."

I catch the word hope as it comes out of my mouth. She does, too, and she chuckles. "Have a good day," she says, then thanks me in return.

CHAPTER 3

ROSALIE

I expect Jay to say something as we walk toward my friends, but he doesn't. He just marches along like a dutiful soldier. Like I'm being escorted in some official capacity. Like we're going through prescripted motions. It's strange. I like walking next to him, though. I catch myself thinking about his muscular shoulders and what they must look like underneath his shirt.

I practically have to slap myself to snap out of it.

"Um, these are my friends, Clara and Ella," I say to him as I disperse the drinks.

"Hi!" Clara chirps.

"What's up?" Ella asks. I swear, she sounds like a trucker when she's off the clock.

"Good to meet you," Jay says. He stands with his hands wrapped around his cup. He doesn't reach out to shake.

It's weird and not, all at the same time. Maybe I'm overthinking this. Dude is definitely hot. The silence lasts for more than a minute and is on the verge of becoming awkward when Ella saves the day.

"Do you have a phone number?" she asks Jay, shamelessly.

He stiffens, then turns to look at me. He thinks Ella wants the number for herself. He and I both blush, pink filling our cheeks and radiating down our necks.

"Yeah, I have a phone," he replies.

"A phone number," I correct.

What? Now I'm speaking for him? This is going nowhere fast. I'd like it to go somewhere. Maybe.

He lowers his brow and glances at me again. "Right. I have a phone number." Then he adds, "Who's asking?"

Ella tilts her head to one side as a sly smile spreads across her face. "A fine little deuce caboose that could use derailing, if you get my meaning." She raises one hand in the air and gestures in my direction, emphasizing the point.

At this, Jay bursts into laughter, finally loosening up and showing a glimpse of what I hope is a fun personality. I hope this is the real him, peeking through. Maybe he could take a glance at my deuce caboose. Whatever that means.

"I'm sorry," Jay says through laughter, "What kind of what? Did you say a *deuce caboose*?"

Ella puts a hand on a hip, continuing the demonstration. "You laugh, but you all knew what I meant. But hey, would you rather we discuss her rebel runway? It's ready for a joyride, if you get my drift."

Jay doubles over laughing so hard that tears stream down his cheeks. Clara and I are used to Ella's shenanigans, but they're all new to him. Apparently, he finds my friend hilarious.

"Excuse her," I say with a smile. "Ella's … one of a kind."

"That's an understatement," Clara adds.

"Am I?" Ella asks playfully. "Or are we all horny?"

Feeling looser, Jay asks, "the three of you? Horny for each other? You are beautiful ladies. I might like to get in on some of that action."

Clara looks like she might faint. She fans her face with one hand.

I chuckle, deciding to make light of it. "We might be horny, but we're not *that* kind of friends," I say.

Ella licks her lips seductively. "We could be," she purrs.

We search each other's eyes for the truth. We *think* Ella is kidding. Is she kidding?

Jay touches my shoulder casually as we laugh together, and a tiny jolt moves through me. His hand is strong. For a second, I imagine him laying his strong hands all over me. My rebel runway would surely enjoy those hands.

It has been too long since a man placed his hands on me.

Motivated by like—or lust—I gather my courage and do the asking. "Hey, I'd like your phone number. If you might want to get together sometime," I say, a lump forming in my throat as I await his response.

He stops and looks me in the eye without awkwardness for the first time. "Yeah, that would be great," he says.

I lower my head bashfully, my eyes meeting his. When we don't seal the deal right away, Ella steps in, again.

"Okay, I guess I have to walk you two through this," she says. "Have a pen?"

I left my handbag at my desk. Clara and Ella don't have theirs either, so I assume they did the same. Jay pauses, then seems to suddenly remember a writing implement in one of his pockets.

"I have a Sharpie!" he exclaims, holding it up like he's found buried treasure. "But I don't have paper," he adds, dismayed.

Ella shakes her head, then points to the paper cup in my hand. "Write it there," she says, gesturing.

Following instructions, Jay scribbles his phone number on my cup. We both smile timidly when our hands touch.

"I'll call you," I say.

For a split second, I wonder if I should have given him my number instead. Must the men do the calling in this modern day and age? That's an old fashioned notion, right? I quickly forget about it because Jay flashes a smile, then walks away.

"See ya," he says.

"Toodaloo," I reply, immediately regretting it.

Oh, well.

As he leaves, I take my time and admire the view. He's put together nicely, that's for sure. I'd like to see him wearing less. Maybe I will. Soon.

When I look back at my friends, Ella winks at me, as if she knew exactly what I needed. She made us all laugh in a few minutes flat. Now we're ready to face the camera crew, our bond of friendship a buoy.

For now, we'll ignore the reference to becoming a different sort of friends.

"Thank you," I say softly as I gather myself and refocus on the day ahead.

Clara giggles. Ella winks again.

At the same time, Sonny returns with an air of confident determination. "Ready, ladies?" he asks as he pops a mint into his mouth. Two guys behind him sling cameras onto their shoulders.

I shake my limbs like a boxer before a fight, tilting my head from side to side. "We're ready," I say.

"Great," Sonny replies. "Let's do a few shots here in the lobby, then we'll move to the flower shop. The light is perfect there this time of morning."

"Okay," I say.

"Is your assistant ready?" he asks.

I glance back at Rachael, who immediately shows us a toothy grin. She must have watched the whole thing play out with Jay.

Oh, my. Moving on.

"Yep, she's ready, too," I reply. "Draw us like one of your French girls."

Sonny pauses, then chuckles.

"Do you get the reference?" Clara asks. "Rosalie loves old movies. She likes to quote them every chance she gets."

"She doesn't need you to speak for her," Ella says.

"You mean the way you spoke for her earlier?" Clara asks. "Hypocrite, much?"

I lower my brows, put my hands on my hips, and give them a look of warning. What have we gotten ourselves into? I hope we don't bicker on camera.

"Ladies, hush," I say.

You know, maybe a little sexy time would ease the tension. A flash of Jay's strong physique enters my mind's eye, and I'm not ashamed to admit that I might like to imagine more.

Okay, stop it, I tell myself. *Focus.*

I'm feeling … pressure … between my legs. I might need to make a quick pit stop in the bathroom to relieve it. I can't believe I'm actually thinking that, but I am.

"Oh, I get the reference," Sonny confirms with a laugh. "*Titanic* is one of my favorites. Although, as far as I'm concerned, movies from the 90s aren't old. Not for an aging geezer like me."

We laugh, nervous energy threatening to rear its head again. It doesn't, though. We can do this. We have what it takes. We're ready.

As soon as I … relieve myself.

"Excuse me," I say, hoping the urgency isn't obvious in my voice. "I need to, um, make a trip to the ladies' room. To powder my nose. I'll be back as fast as I can."

I don't have my handbag. No powder. *Whatever.* That excuse is as good as any.

The others politely agree to wait. A quick glance at the guys with cameras on their shoulders make it seem like they're still making adjustments to their equipment.

"Take your time," Sonny offers.

I shimmy off to the ladies' room, my heels tapping

furiously against the concrete floors. I feel Ella watching me. I don't turn back. Whatever is happening isn't something I'm ready to acknowledge to myself, let alone discuss with anyone else.

Maybe it's nerves, what with the filming and camera crew. All I know is that my body is desperate, aching for a release.

When I get inside the bathroom, I latch and lock the heavy door behind me. I lean back against it, one hand reaching hungrily beneath my blouse for a firm, protruding nipple and the other slipping up my skirt and underneath my lace panties. My pleasure petals are absolutely drenched with desire. My fingers slip and slide as they caress the folds.

The bathroom is a small room designated as unisex. There aren't dividers and there's nowhere for anyone else to hide. I'm certain I'm alone. I can let myself go.

I close my eyes, and I see Jay. He's wearing nothing but gray athletic shorts in my fantasy, an expansive bulge rising to greet me. I finger myself harder, the ripple of his chest muscles looking positively scrumptious. I arch my back as the feelings of pleasure become more and more intense. I lick my lips, imagining what his mouth will taste like pressed against mine. I roll my fingers, imagining what his body will feel like to touch. I finger my nipple harder, the fabric of my blouse rubbing against it and driving my passion higher and higher.

I'm writhing with desire, pleasure already coursing through every inch of my body, when suddenly, fantasy Jay strips off his shorts and is completely naked. The image pops into my mind like a Christmas-morning surprise. I didn't ask for it. I didn't conjure it or summon it, but it's here.

He stretches out on his side, the bed in my apartment becoming the backdrop. His muscles look delicious, and I find myself wanting to touch them. To feel his firm, warm skin on my own.

I rub harder, faster, grabbing at myself greedily, my hands glossy with bliss. I give in to my fantasy and where my passions want to take me. I give in to my lust for Jay. I imagine us entwined, his plump lips on mine, my taut nipples brushing against his chest, my … tickler … sliding around him in the most titillating way. I rock and bang against the bathroom door so hard that I think it might come off its hinges.

When I climax, I swear, it's like nothing I've ever experienced before. It feels as if my entire body explodes into a beautiful, savory vigor for life itself. *Ahh.* That's what I needed. That hits the spot—quite literally.

I just hope no one is on the other side of the bathroom door. I hope no one heard me moaning and wailing like an untamed, wild woman. Because I was definitely moaning and wailing like an untamed, wild woman.

"Fuck!" I exclaim.

When I begin to cool down, a sharp knock on the other side of the door tells me that my little adventure hasn't gone unnoticed.

"Rosie? Are you okay in there?"

It's Clara, of all people. "Be right out," I say as I use one arm to wipe perspiration from my brow.

My voice is breathy. My legs shake from the exertion.

"Are you hurt?" she asks. "Did something happen? I thought I heard you crying."

I laugh, small chuckles quickly growing into loud belly laughs. I look down at my rumpled clothes and my wet hands, and I find the absurdity of the situation hilarious. I was all put together for filming. Now I'm all torn apart. Even my hair is disheveled, although I'm not completely sure how it got that way. I must have run my fingers through it.

"Are you … laughing?" Clara asks in disbelief, trying to make sense of what she's heard.

"I'm laughing," I reply. "I am *laughing!*"

I lean back hard against the door. Suddenly, the latch lets go and it swings open. Unable to catch my balance in time, I tumble into the lobby. I roll, my feet careening over my head while my skirt—and my legs—fly wide open. Everyone in the lobby is treated to a generous view.

No one says a word for what feels like an excruciating length of time.

I'm mortified, but I'm still laughing. I can't help myself. "Um, yeah," I finally manage. "Is this natural enough for you?"

"Rosie," Ella whispers, "look." She gestures to the cameras that are, apparently, rolling.

Kill me now. I sure hope they didn't get all of that on film.

"Oh, wow," I say. "This is unfortunate."

Sunny looks amused. He nods at his crew, as if to say they're keeping the footage, whether I like it or not.

On second thought, who cares if they did record my … event?

The people in this crew don't know my story. They don't know what I've been through or how it's affected me. They don't know that I'm finally coming back to life.

CHAPTER 4

ROSALIE

Three Days Later

It's day four of filming, and I'm much more at ease than I was when we began. It's remarkable how quickly you can get used to a camera crew following you around. Sonny and his team have been camped out in my flower shop for so many hours that I hardly notice them now.

The cameras almost blend in among the lush bunches of flowers. Kind of like E.T. on the bed of stuffed animals. That was one of my mom's favorite old movies. Thinking about it brings a smile to my face.

Rachael seems used to the cameras, too.

She and I are chatting casually as we work, doing our best to act natural and pretend the cameras aren't here. Clara and Ella are in their offices, enjoying a break from filming while waiting their turns.

I prompt myself to come up with a topic of conversation that might be interesting for the film crew.

Think. Say something. Anything.

"Patrick Hart was the worst," I say glumly. "He and his brother Jesse used to tease me something awful when we were kids. I can practically taste the warm, salty tears I had to bite back on a regular basis."

Rachael raises her brows. "That's random," she replies.

Sonny instructed us to make smalltalk. This topic seems as good as any other.

"It was pitiful," I continue as I sip a cup of lukewarm tea I bought from Hope on my way in this morning. "I would fume, sad and alone in the bathroom stall at Loveland Elementary. I'm surprised I didn't turn royal blue, what with all the time I spent sobbing against that painted metal door." I wring my hands as I talk, forgetting about the film crew and beginning to feel uncomfortable in my skin. "The woeful scene always took place in stall number five. The one farthest away from the entrance. The one I deemed most likely to keep me hidden from the prying eyes of my classmates."

"Okay, now that's random *and* sad," Rachael adds. She forms her painted, cherry-red lips into a sympathetic pout. "You poor thing. I'm sorry."

I ramble on, caught up in my own childhood drama. "Maybe I deserved it. My parents did name me Rosalie Flowers, after all. I mean, what did they think kids on the grade school playground would do with that name? It's so damn syrupy sweet. It begs for attention."

"I don't know," Rachael muses as she runs a hand through her artfully tousled long hair. "I think it suits you."

"I appreciate that," I say. "But if I'd been in charge of the naming, I would have given my daughter a strong, solid first name to balance out the ultra-feminine last name Flowers. Maybe something badass like Drew or Riley."

"Or something simple like Emily or Sarah. Or Rachael," she adds.

"Exactly!" I reply, happy that she gets it. "Rachael is a beautiful name. But nope. Rosalie it is. How ... *sweet*."

"Yeah."

I take a breath, then continue. "In middle school, things only got worse. Young Patrick made a point to tell everyone how ugly I was compared to a real rose. He said I was skin and bones, more like the thorny parts without the pretty bloom up top."

"Ouch," she replies. "That was uncalled for. Are you sure he was talking about ... ?" She gestures at her own blooms, cupping her hands and hoisting them upward.

Sonny's team is probably loving the hands-on demo. I can imagine the zoom action that will, no doubt, wind up in the final cut. I won't blame them. I'm sure this makes for good television.

I nod, my upper lip stiffening. "He didn't have to spell it out any further. I knew what he meant. It was a dig at my slow-to-develop physique. And he was right. My girls hadn't— well, bloomed— yet. I was as flat chested as the day is long."

She smiles sympathetically. "What a brat."

"Being flat-chested was embarrassing," I explain. "So totally embarrassing. Dressing out for gym class usually caused me to break into a cold sweat. When it came time to change alongside the other more voluminous girls, I couldn't stuff myself far enough into the corner of the locker room. I'd have crawled right inside a locker, if that had been a viable option. The space was too tight to cram my body into. Believe me, I tried."

"Rosalie," Rachael says, attempting to interrupt my downward spiral, "you're a grown woman with a solid sense of self-esteem now. That mess is in the past."

She grabs a clean cloth from under the counter and begins to polish an elegant glass vase while we chat. She looks kind of like a bartender, absentmindedly polishing away while she listens to my woes.

"I know. The, um, *bloom situation* eventually changed for the better. It may have taken a while, but I blossomed beautifully, if I do say so myself."

"I can see that," she confirms with a chuckle.

"Humph!" I huff. "Better late than never."

"Absolutely."

I grab a cloth and a vase, too, and begin to polish. "These days," I add, "I consider my ample blooms one of my best physical assets. I suppose it's true what they say about good things coming to those who wait. There are dozens of girls I know who budded early, then stopped short before reaching my level of pleasing roundness and exquisite, busty bulk."

Rachael tilts her head to one side. "Are you trying to convince me, or yourself?" she asks. "Because that's quite a description there, Shakespeare."

Her silver ring with tiny diamonds sparkles as her hand moves and the light catches it. She wears the ring on her left hand where an engagement ring would normally be placed, but she's as single as I am. She claims it was a gift for her college graduation. It seems like there's more to the story, and I'm tempted to ask. I'm still wrapped up in my own drama, though. I'm not quite ready to change the subject.

"Silly Patrick. Screw him," I practically spit. "What does he know about me, really? For that matter, why am I even thinking about him? I surely have better, more productive tasks to focus on."

"Sure, you do," Rachael replies.

My flower shop stays busy, as evidenced by the colorful, delicate beauties all around us. Business awaits.

"Hey, did you call Jay yet?" she asks. "I know you're playing hard to get, but hasn't it been long enough?"

I shrug, not sure that I'm playing hard to get. I'm also not sure I want to discuss it. "I called," I say.

"And?"

"And we have a date next Friday night."

She smiles, and I can tell she wants to celebrate with me. "Look at you," she says enthusiastically. "Going on a da-ate with a bo-oy."

"He's a full grown man," I say, my mood dampened by thoughts of my childhood tormentors.

"Of course," she replies. "I didn't mean …"

"I know."

"I'm butting in," she says, taking a step back.

I sigh. I shouldn't have snapped at her. "It isn't you," I say. "I'm sorry for being short. Maybe I'm worried that

I'll screw things up. As long as the date is a hypothetical, out in the future, I can enjoy the what-ifs. Once it becomes real, the relationship might come to an end."

"Before it even begins?" she asks.

"Precisely," I reply. "I don't have the best track record. Like, not at all."

A bell rings, announcing a new arrival. I'm grateful for the diversion. The visitor is a tall, extremely handsome man I noticed a few moments ago when he pulled into the parking lot and got out of his car. My pulse quickens.

"We have company," I say.

"I noticed," Rachael says. "You did, too. You're doing that thing with your hands."

"What thing?" I ask.

"You know the thing," she says.

I shrug off her remark, drop my arms, and let my hands relax at my sides. "Fine. How could I *not* notice this guy?" I ask. "He looks striking enough to play Superman if Henry Cavill decides to pass the torch—err … cape. But it doesn't matter. He's probably here to pick out something for his fiancé. This isn't exactly a hot spot for eligible bachelors, in case you hadn't noticed."

"Mm hmm," she mumbles as she smiles. Finished with the first vase, she moves it to a clear spot on the table then pulls another one out to polish. "You met Jay here, just the other day," she adds.

"A fluke," I whisper, then wave her off.

I take a few steps forward to greet our new arrival. "Welcome! Come on in," I say as he steps inside. "Don't mind the cameras. They're filming for a TV series."

He's camera ready, if ever a man was.

Damn. He looks good. Um, um, umh.

He smiles politely in our direction, but doesn't make direct eye contact. He seems distracted. "Okay, yeah. Thanks."

It's been raining on and off all day. "Bad weather," I say, turning back to Rachael. "I drove in to work today, and the roads were a mess."

"Uh huh," she says.

The man shakes the water out of a short black umbrella then sets it down in the metal bin next to the front door. The umbrella clanks pleasantly as it hits. "Someone left this on the sidewalk out front," he says. "They probably dropped it and didn't realize it was missing. Thought I'd bring it in, out of the rain."

"Nice," I say, enjoying a chance to gaze at him.

My—um, *pleasure petals*—are beginning to tingle.

It *was* nice of him to bring the umbrella inside. A lot of people would have left the thing out there to float away. It's always good to see someone taking time for neighborly gestures.

The man nods, then hesitates. "Wait a minute," he mumbles, and I assume he has forgotten something in his car. His phone, maybe? He turns to one side, his shoulders hunched.

"Take your time," I say. "We aren't going anywhere. Well, not until five o'clock, anyway." I laugh nervously, lifting my hands again and lacing my fingers together.

I don't want him to leave my shop. Not until I can get a better look at him. Maybe a sniff.

That sounds weird, I know. But I'll bet he smells

amazing. He's clean cut and sort of polished in that rugged way that drives me completely wild. He, seriously, would make a good Superman. I'll be his Lois Lane.

I turn to Rachael for support. All she offers is a sheepish smile and a "yep, five o'clock," as she glances at my hands.

The man doesn't seem to be paying attention. He turns his back to us and stares out the front window. From his dress and demeanor, I'd guess he's some sort of professional. "Probably a doctor or lawyer. Or a financial advisor," I whisper to Rachael.

She nods.

Funny that I haven't seen him around, though. Loveland is a small town. I'm fairly certain I could name all of the male doctors, lawyers, and financial advisors. There's Dr. Dickson, Dr. Tate, Dr. Wong … I stop myself there. None of them are as young as this guy. Or as handsome. He must be new.

Focus, I tell myself.

I must be smiling obnoxiously because Rachael is eyeing me. "Easy, girl," she says with a grin. "You already have one on the hook."

That's true. I do.

"Oh, be quiet."

I'll admit, I find a well dressed man incredibly appealing. There's something about seeing an attractive man outfitted in nice clothing that turns me on. It becomes a quest of sorts to get the fancy man out of his fancy clothes and see what he looks like wearing nothing at all. Once that happens, I feel lucky to have seen the secret physique that lies hidden from—humor me—all of the other women in the world.

"Are you here to pick up a flower arrangement?" I ask the man, giving him a chance to say more. "Did you order ahead?"

My voice is strong. I project, to be sure he can hear me all the way at the front of the store. The place isn't huge, but it isn't small, either. Besides, Sonny likes me to speak up for the cameras.

The man turns to face us again, then narrows his eyes and raises one strong hand to his chin. That chin is so chiseled it could probably cut glass. An image of him sliding it along my inner thigh pops into my head.

Oh, boy.

My pleasure petals are positively buzzing. I cross my legs at the ankles, as if I can make the feeling stop. As if I'd *want to* make the feeling stop.

"Um," he says, clearing his throat, "is it okay if I look around for a few minutes?"

"Of course," I reply. "Help yourself."

He smiles politely, then glides along the front of the store by the windows, his gaze tracing the lines of the building. It's odd, but I let it go. Whatever.

Slowly, I make my way to a stool closer to Rachael and sit. "What's up?" she asks, knowing that I have plenty to say.

I shake my head. "Those Hart brothers I was telling you about—"

"Oh, we're talking about this again?" she asks.

My stare tells her that we are, in fact, talking about this again.

"Right," she says. "Patrick and Jesse?"

"Yeah," I reply, my voice low. "They moved away from Loveland the summer before our freshman year of high school."

"How come?" she asks.

"Their parents divorced, and their mom married a wealthy businessman in Atlanta. I'd heard rumors the boys wanted to stick around here with their dad, but no such luck. It didn't work out that way. For better or worse, they were sent off to live a life in the big city."

"Nashville wasn't big enough?" she asks.

"Maybe not. Or maybe the stepdad was from Atlanta. I don't know all of the details," I explain.

"Huh."

"I was a little envious of their newfound proximity to everything that seemed worldly and exciting—especially at that age. I remember the 1996 Olympics taking place in Atlanta when we were young kids. If that isn't worldly, I don't know what is."

"True. I'll give you that."

"But mostly, I was glad they were gone," I continue. "I can't imagine the move helped Patrick's attitude any. The rat race that is Atlanta probably made him even more arrogant than he was before."

"Not all big city people are rude," Rachael says. "That's a stereotype that doesn't always match up to real life."

"Yeah, but Atlanta is different from other big cities, right?" I ask. "It's certainly different from Nashville. I mean, let's call it what it likely was—a cocoon filled with fellow pretentious wannabes. I'll bet it was the perfect environment for Patrick to come of age in all his smug, pathetic glory."

Ew. The thought makes me disgusted.

Rachael grunts, polishing away like a good bartender.

"I can see him now," I say, "schmoozing his way through his teenage years while being an ass to some other poor girl who happened to find herself in his line of fire. Not to wish bad things on anyone else, but I sure was happy to be rid of those troublesome Hart brothers. My life improved exponentially when they got the hell out of dodge."

"This is a sore subject for you, isn't it?" Rachael asks.

"I don't know if it's a sore subject, exactly," I say, barely skipping a beat. "But without Patrick and Jesse as ringleaders egging others on, the kids at school left me in peace. It was a sweet, blessed relief."

"Just so you know," she says playfully, "I'm not a trained therapist. Although, I feel like I should be charging by the hour."

I look at her and laugh. "Can I afford you?"

"Probably not."

Wait. She raises a good point. Why am I thinking about those little creeps all these years later when I'm a grown woman with a mostly happy life?

"Sorry," I say.

"No worries," she replies. "You're acting kind of weird. That's all."

Am I? I'm feeling kind of weird. Not as weird as on day one of filming.

So, there's that.

I glance over at Sonny. He and his boys have multiple cameras scanning the room. If I spent much time worrying about them, I'd surely go insane by the end of the ten months they'll be here. I remind myself to ignore them. Although, I make a mental note to have our handsome customer sign a release in case Sonny wants to use footage showing his face.

I shrug. "I don't know why I'm talking about Patrick and Jesse Hart. It's ancient history."

"Um hmm," Rachael says again, clearly not convinced.

The man paces in the front of my store, almost like he's working up the nerve for something. Which doesn't make any sense. When do Superman types get nervous? Does that even happen? Maybe what we're seeing is the Clark Kent version.

"What made you think of Patrick and Jesse, anyway?" Rachael asks.

"You know, I'm honestly not sure," I say. "I haven't thought of them in years."

Rachael nods. "You've never mentioned them to me. Something must have brought them to mind."

I toss my head to one side as I raise my hands, then lower them.

Then, like a freight train on a runaway track, it hits me. "Oh," I say, my jaw dropping.

She stops polishing and leans forward. "Oh … what? This sounds like it's gonna be good."

I suddenly know exactly why those pesky brothers came to mind.

Because I'm pretty sure the tall, handsome man pacing up front actually *is* Patrick Hart, in the flesh, here in my shop. He's older, and thicker—in a good way—but it's him.

Oh.My.God.

I stand, my eyes wide. Rachael looks at me expectantly. Before I can get any coherent speech out, Patrick walks toward us, clamoring on about something. He doesn't seem to know who I am. But I know who he is, and I'm too stunned to process his words in real time.

I go weak in the knees when he hands me his card and I read the name printed neatly in block letters on the front.

It's really him. Patrick M. Hart.

I nod and smile graciously as he chatters away and the room spins at what feels like hyper speed. Out of the corner of one eye, I glance around my shop, mapping escape routes. If only my limbs hadn't turned to useless rubber. I quickly come to the realization that there's no escape.

Patrick's here to tell me that his company has been hired to renovate the building. He's an architect, and looking at him up close, he's … dreamy. Dark hair. That strong jawline. Big, broad shoulders. Smoldering blue eyes. A jovial smile that makes me wonder if he's undressing me with those eyes. Or if I want him to.

I haven't told him my name yet. I honestly don't think he knows it's me. He's settling now, seeming at ease.

I've got to buy myself some time.

The man standing in front of me doesn't begin to match up with my memory of the scrawny kid from school. His entire vibe is ... different. Much better. Much more appealing. *This* man is making me perspire.

It just got flaming hot in here.

CHAPTER 5

PATRICK

I knew. Don't hate me.

I've been back in Loveland for several months, and I'm well aware that Rosalie still lives here. In fact, she's one of the reasons I decided to leave Atlanta and join my father's small-town firm.

That professional step has been a long time coming. The moment I declared architecture as my major at the University of Georgia, it was inevitable that I would someday return to Loveland and work with my dad. The two of us have a complicated history, but all in all, this move is a good thing for long term father-son bonding. Dad is getting to the ripe old age where he's beginning to think about his legacy. It's important to him that I be a part of that legacy, if I have any interest whatsoever in doing so.

I did. *I do.* Especially considering his recent health scare. Thankfully, his disease is in remission. He's all good. What better time to look toward a bright future?

So, I made the move.

Now, here I am, staring Rosalie dead in the eyes and pretending I don't know who she is ... on camera, no less. No wonder it took me a few beats to collect myself when I first entered her shop. Seeing her in person after all these years was overwhelming.

My best bud, Brandon Dobson, warned me that it would be tough. I guess I should've listened to his sage advice. So, what if we were both three sheets to the wind when he doled out his wisdom last winter?

"Move back to Loveland," he said. "You're pushing thirty. If you want to settle down and have kids, you had better do it sooner rather than later."

"What makes you think my future wife is in Loveland, of all places?" I asked.

"Seriously?" he replied.

"Hey now," I said. "I told you that in confidence. Not so you could throw it in my face when you want me to get out so you can find a new roommate. I know it's all about the hefty rate you're going to charge the next S.O.B. who bunks with you. You want me out so a new guy—or girl—can slide in and pay top dollar for these digs. You're making me feel icky, you money-grubber, you."

At this, he laughed raucously. "You crack me up when you talk like that, bro."

I laughed, too. "All part of my master plan. I have to keep you on your toes."

His long, brush-shaped mustache moved as he took a swig of his craft beer, looking every bit the part of a college-town hipster. Brandon never did seem like he fit in the ritzy Atlanta neighborhood of Buckhead. Not that I did, either, but at that moment it seemed like my friend should be moving to Loveland with me. Small-town Tennessee life would probably suit him.

I dropped to the other end of the leather sofa he was lounging on and gave him a serious stare. "Come with me," I said.

"What?" he asked.

Earlier that day, we'd helped a pregnant woman whose water had broken on the MARTA train as we pulled into Lenox Station. Her contractions had been coming hard and fast, and she'd been all alone on her morning commute. Brandon and I had helped her call her husband and her mom, then we had accompanied her to the hospital where we'd waited until her family arrived. Maybe that was why the subject of our own futures had surfaced.

"Come with me," I said. "To Loveland. We'll both move there. We can be roommates, if you want, or we can each get our own place. It's cheap enough for either setup. Compared to the way we exist in this concrete jungle, we could live like kings. No joke."

He leaned his head back, like a turtle collapsing into itself. "Dude, I've lived in Atlanta all my life. I've never even thought about leaving."

"You're pushing thirty, too," I said.

"So?"

"So, don't you want a family of your own? You always talk about having kids one day. You'd be a good dad, Brandon."

He nodded. "So would you," he replied. "Scratch that. So *will* you."

I smiled, then took a sip of my own beer, pondering what the future might hold for the two of us.

Maverick, my hounddog, rolled over and groaned, as if on cue. I'd been meaning to get that big guy out of the city in favor of someplace with wide open spaces. Piedmont Park is nice, but it's usually crowded. Pets aren't allowed in the park's lake, and I know Mav would dig swimming.

It's a strange thing to reach a point where having a family moves to the top of your to-do list. Ten years ago, as a kid fresh out of high school, it was the last thing on my mind. I had wild oats to sow. Goals to crush. Challenges to conquer. Now? I'm not going to lie. Having a family is on my radar.

"That went deep," my friend said as he ran one finger over the rim of his bottle. City lights twinkled outside our paned window, casting a thoughtful glow on Brandon's face. "I'm not sure how things got turned around in my direction. You're the one pining for Rosalie Flowers. I'm simply the friend telling you to go after what you want. How does that land *me* in Loveland?"

I shrugged. "I don't know, man. Maybe I'm deflecting. Don't get me wrong. Having my best friend in town would be outstanding. I'd love it if you made the move along with me. If I do it, that is."

"If? Okay. Tell yourself that," he said.

I sighed and closed my eyes, thinking about Rosalie.

I knew it was a stretch to believe we could be together. We'd had zero contact since middle school. Middle school! Yet, I'd inadvertently kept tabs on her while keeping up with happenings and news in my hometown. I'm only a little embarrassed to admit that I have a file on my laptop with Rosalie images I've saved over the years. Every time I've come across a new public picture of her, I've saved it.

Even when I've dated other women, Rosalie was never far from my mind.

Something about Rosalie Flowers took hold of me way back when we were kids, and it hasn't let go.

Brandon interrupted my train of thought. "You're thinking of her. Aren't you?"

A smile formed on my lips without my permission. I couldn't help it. "Maybe," I replied.

"Maybe, my ass," he said with a grin. Then, after a pause, "tell me more about her."

"Nah," I said, "it's silly. She was my first crush. That's all. Life moved on."

He leaned toward me, making it clear that he wouldn't take no for an answer. "Don't do that. Tell me. What is she like?"

"You really want to know?"

He nods.

"Okay, then. Fuck it," I replied. I stood, then grabbed my laptop from my bedroom and brought it back to the sofa. "I'll show you the website for the flower shop she owns—Rosalie's Flowers. You can see for yourself."

"Let's do it," he replied, taking another swig of beer.

I pulled up the website in less than a minute. I knew the url, of course, because I've visited the site before. Rosalie writes a blog about her business adventures, and I enjoy reading her posts. Her website is professional and elegant.

"Here she is," I said as I tilted the screen for Brandon to see my girl's stunning face. "Sweet Rosalie. She's prettier than any flower in her shop, that's for damn sure."

Brandon looked hard at her, then took the computer onto his own lap and navigated the main pages on her website. He moved slowly and deliberately, with an air of respect. I appreciated that. I felt ridiculous enough as it was.

"She's strong in a quiet way, without being overbearing," I explained, "as if she's an old, wise soul. She's smart as a whip, too. She used to run circles around me in pretty much every academic subject. I remember watching her like a hawk—when she wasn't aware, of course. She was always the first to finish her work in class or to raise her hand when a teacher asked a question. I remember looking for her name on the honor roll. It was always there, without fail."

"Yeah?"

"Don't get me started on how pretty she is. I mean, you can see that for yourself. Just look at her! She's my ideal woman. In every way," I said, gesturing at the screen. I sounded like a hopeless romantic. It was odd, being so enamored with another person.

"Dude, what's stopping you?" Brandon asked.

I scoffed. "You ask, like it's a normal thing to upend my entire life to chase a woman I haven't seen since I was a pimple-faced kid. Who does that?"

"True," he said. "But that doesn't mean you shouldn't try."

"Plus," I continued, "I'm sure Rosalie has no shortage

of admirers beating down her door. Hell, back in the day, I think my brother even had a crush on her."

"JT?" Brandon asked. "Really?"

"He went by Jesse back then, but yeah, the one and only," I replied. "Not to mention, we picked on her because we were too young and stupid to realize how much we actually liked her. For all I know, she hates us both."

Brandon raised his brows. "Huh."

I paused for a moment, took another swig of beer, then decided to change my tone. "This is crazy. Forget I said anything about Rosalie," I muttered as I stood and paced the floor. "My dad's health situation is reason enough to consider the move home. That's what I should be talking about. We dodged a bullet on that one. I don't want to waste any more time."

Brandon nodded. "I get it. Have you heard details about his prognosis?"

I shook my head. "Just that he's in remission, which is all I need to hear. He's still frail and is supposed to take it easy for a while, but his prognosis is good."

Brandon leaned over and put a reassuring hand on my shoulder. "I'm relieved with you, buddy. It sounds like Daddio is going to be just fine. I know you've thought about moving back home to work with him. Maybe the timing is right."

I nodded. "Agreed. Changes are coming. Big ones. I can feel it. Dad's digging into his vision for the future—he's talking about investments and buyouts and all sorts of business moves that sound risky to me. How will he do any of that without my help, given the fact that he isn't back to full strength? I want to be there for him."

A long silence stretched between us. There was so much to say, so much to consider. Although, a ton of words weren't necessary.

"I'm here," Brandon said. "Whatever you need. Don't hesitate to ask."

"I appreciate it, my friend," I replied, and I meant it. "You and old Maverick here are my best buds. I don't know what I'd do without you."

Maverick groaned again, his lips curling into what looked like a sly smile. Brandon gave me a wink, then shared a knowing glance with the dog.

Family and friends—the hounddog included—are what life's all about. I'm grateful for mine.

Then and now.

As I stand in Rosalie's flower shop, still damp from the downpour, that winter conversation with Brandon in our Buckhead apartment seems a million miles away. So much has happened since then. With the move. With Dad.

After I arrived in Loveland, I waited a while before approaching Rosalie.

I thought about calling her, so it would be easier for her to bow out gracefully if she wasn't interested. I even thought about calling one of her friends to gauge their opinion on whether I should reach out.

Once I heard that Dad's firm—*our* firm—was handling the renovation of the building she's buying, I knew it was time to get serious. Especially once I heard Dad's plans for the property. He wants it for himself.

I'm not sure how I'll do it without anyone I care about getting hurt, but at some point I might need to intervene.

I smile at Rosalie, all the while telling myself to play it cool and not act like a total oaf.

I feel bad, pretending I don't know who she is.

Well, a little bit bad. *Okay, fine.* Not that bad. If I can somehow win her over, it will all have been worth it. My gut will have been right.

It's time to do this.

CHAPTER 6

ROSALIE

"*M*a'am?" Patrick asks, his voice smooth like warm butter.

I'd be insulted that he called me ma'am—aren't I too young for that?—but I remember that his dad is from the Deep South. I'm pretty sure they consider ma'am appropriate for ladies of any age. At least, I hope so. Otherwise, how old does Patrick think I am?

I straighten the waistband on my pink satin skirt while deciding whether to be offended. I can feel his gaze on me as the curve-hugging material bounces around my hips, thanks to the deep pleats. *Oops.* I wasn't trying to be flirty. Or at least, that's what I tell myself. Now that I think of it, my white lace shirt clings in all the right places, too.

I hear a whirring sound from one of the cameras that I'm sure is a zoom function.

"Yes," I manage to reply. "The building. Yes. You're here to renovate it. I mean, not renovate it today. You know … um, yeah. When it's time." I smile. "You. Building. Check."

It's an old factory building with sky-high ceilings and exposed brick. It's charming now, and I imagine it will be drop-dead gorgeous after the reno. I can hardly wait. I hope the finished product lives up to the inspo I've saved to my Pinterest board. You can bet I'll soon be blowing up social media with before-and-after images, as one does.

My business goals are all coming to fruition, right before my eyes. I've long dreamt of owning and growing a meaningful part of this little town. Being in a business that brings happiness to people is icing on the cake. One day, I hope to pass a nest egg on to my kids.

I'm getting way ahead of myself. First, I need a boyfriend. Come to think of it, I might be too old to use the term boyfriend. What am I, twelve? Decidedly not. So, what should I call my future boy toy? My partner? My love interest? My significant other? *Whatever*. That's a problem for another day.

"Good," Patrick says as he reaches towards me with a manilla envelope in one hand. "All the information you'll need is right here. We aim to keep disruptions to a minimum."

"Good," I echo, taking the envelope from him.

I try to say something more eloquent, but the words seem to be jumbled up in my mouth, suddenly an alphabet soup. I look at Patrick's lips. They're pink and plump. They look delectable.

Oh, no. He notices me looking at them. Busted.

How embarrassing. Not as embarrassing as busting

out of the bathroom door with my hand practically in my panties the other day, but still embarrassing.

Speaking of the other day, I don't mean to sound petty because I know looks aren't everything, but Patrick is way hotter than Jay from the coffee stand. Not that Jay isn't hot. He was. He *is*! Hot enough to be— um, inspirational. Remember?

But Patrick is something else.

Um, mm, mmh! Emphasis on the *mmh!*

"Ma'am, are you okay?" Patrick asks.

"Um …" I mumble.

This isn't going well. It's going horribly, truth be told. I'm conflicted.

Patrick was the bane of my existence. I hated him. With a passion. If my mama would have let me make a voodoo doll, it would have been of Patrick. So why am I feeling … this way about him now?

This is weird. I feel weird. Maybe I am weird.

Get it together, Rosalie.

"I'm okay," I say, avoiding eye contact.

"That's good," he replies.

Between the two of us, we're going to wear that word out. Everything is, apparently, good.

"Is it still raining out there?" I ask, immediately regretting it. Of course, it's raining out there. It's springtime in Middle Tennessee. *Duh.* Not to mention, I can plainly see the rain out the window.

Patrick chuckles as he nods. "Yeah, it is."

This is awkward.

He knows I'm flustered. Maybe he's a little flustered, too, for some strange reason. Maybe my spastic energy is contagious? Not that I'm a good judge of such matters at the moment. Or ever. Most importantly, though, he doesn't recognize me yet. I've got to get out of here before he figures it out.

"Umm …" I mumble. "Right."

The trouble is, I have twenty floral centerpieces to assemble for Saturday's wedding out at the Chestnut Hill Lodge. Even though it's the busy season for us wedding pros and I can't always handle every event personally, I don't think the bride-to-be would appreciate me bailing on this job. I promised her I'd be there, in person. Plus, Rachael is a huge help, but she isn't a miracle worker. I've got to stick around and do my part, unless and until I hire someone else to fill in.

Loveland is a small town and a resort destination. My good reputation is my greatest asset. Not just to me, but to Clara, Ella, and every future wedding professional who joins The Romantics.

That's right!

I suddenly remember, my distracted brain sluggish, but functional. Clara and Ella know Patrick. We all went to school together. I need to text the two of them right away.

They're just down the hall. They will never believe that Patrick is standing here in front of me, in the flesh. They'll, no doubt, drop what they're doing and come racing over to get a look for themselves. Maybe they'll want to get a kick or a jab in, too. They're protective of me, and they know how much he tortured my childhood. They were there to watch the carnage unfold firsthand.

"Ma'am, are you sure you're okay?" Patrick asks. "You seem … I don't know, your face is red."

"I'm fine," I say, even though that's not entirely true.

What else am I supposed to say? That I recognize him as my childhood nemesis? That I hate him? That I was just telling Rachael exactly how much I hate him? Or that I'm not sure how to feel about him now that he seems like a nice guy and looks this … good?

I reach into one pocket in my skirt—it has pockets! —and take out my smartphone. I pull up the group text window to message Ella and Clara while attempting to look inconspicuous. I'm not sure anything about me is inconspicuous right now. My belabored brain cells continue to churn around in my head in disorganized fashion, much like the alphabet soup in my mouth.

Oh, no.

Patrick probably saw the sign out front. He must have. Otherwise, how would he have found us? Surely he knows the business name on the front of the building his firm will renovate, right? Wouldn't it have been on some piece of paperwork somewhere? I'm no architect, but that *has* to be part of the necessary prep work.

Patrick's a smart guy. He was sharp when we were kids, and I can see the intelligence in his bright eyes now. If he doesn't already know, it won't take him long to put it all together.

Before I can figure a way out of this most uncomfortable predicament, an odd look washes over his face.

"Wait," Rachael says, her cherry-red lips forming a thoughtful pout, "do you two know each other?"

I'd almost forgotten Rachael was here. Much like she was during the scene with Jay the other day, she's watching it all. Every cringeworthy second. Of course, the cameras are watching, too.

I nod, then shake my head, then nod again.

Like a baby deer standing on its legs for the first time, I lurch forward for no apparent reason. The heel of my shoe twists funny, and it sends me crashing towards the concrete floor in the least graceful way possible. I feel like all elbows and knees as I flail about, forwards then backwards in a clumsy attempt to stay on my feet. As I tumble, I make a mental note to choose softer flooring material for the remodel. Maybe wood, cut into wide planks.

"This can't be happening," I mumble as I grab for something to hold on to, but it's hopeless. The only thing I can get my hands on is a large vase of gardenias sitting on top of the project table. It comes crashing down next to me as I land with a thud, glass shattering and petals ripping. Water sloshes around the beautiful mess. It soaks my silk skirt.

There goes one of the centerpieces. Of course, it would be the gardenias. Damn those delicate beauties. They've been shipped in from California. They're difficult to grow any time of year and are priced at a premium because of it. In May, forget it. They're in high demand and crazy expensive. Not to mention, there's no time to order more before the ceremony on Saturday.

My smartphone leaps out of my hand and slides across the room like a disc in a game of shuffleboard.

The message window is still open, Clara and Ella's names visible at the top.

"Oh, dear," I mumble.

I silently scold myself for the choice of words. *Oh, dear?* Here I've fallen on my ass in front of an incredibly sexy man—who happens to be Patrick Hart—and that's what I say about it? What am I, a 1950s school girl?

I'm not that sweet in real life. Clara might be. But me? Nope.

Patrick tilts his head to one side as he takes in the scene. My phone slows and finally comes to a stop at his feet.

Shit. Shit. Shit.

He'll see Clara and Ella's names and he'll know it's me for sure. There's no hiding now. No bowing out of our bumbling conversation gracefully. No chance to run.

I'm flustered.

I wasn't anywhere near this flustered when I met Jay the other day. Noted. No time to compare and contrast right now, though.

Patrick's trousers grip his body as he squats to pick up the phone, and I suddenly feel flush. If my face was red before, I'm certain it will go up in flames at any moment. His legs appear to be muscular, like a soccer player's. The lighting is too dim for me to make out the details, but I think I glimpse the outline of some serious … *equipment,* if you get my drift.

Oh, dear.

"Clara and Ella … and..." Patrick begins as he holds

my phone out in front of him. He knows the rest. He's toying with me now. He has to be.

I shake my head back and forth hard, as if the motion might make this all go away.

A grin takes over Patrick's strong features and I melt right into the floor, a mixture of attraction and awkwardness swirling between us.

"And Loveland, Tennessee's very own, Rosalie Flowers."

He pauses, for dramatic effect.

"Oh! The brat from middle school," Rachael says with a laugh as she looks on. "Now, I think I've seen it all. This is going to be interesting."

CHAPTER 7

ROSALIE

"That's me," I admit bashfully as Patrick reaches out a hand to help me up. A jolt of electricity courses through my body. "Slippery. It's… slippery," I say.

Slippery? How embarrassing. What am I saying?

Once I'm upright, he places his other strong, firm hand on the small of my back and I think I might just die right here and now. Luckily, the heel on my shoe is intact and will hold me. I was afraid it had broken off.

"Wow," he says with a smile. "You look… Just, wow."

I curtsey in response as Rachael eyes me curiously. She takes a few steps back. Apparently, to give me space.

What am I even doing right now?

Patrick chuckles. He isn't turning away. And he doesn't acknowledge my slippery comment. Maybe I haven't completely blown it for myself.

Except that I hate him. *Dammit.*

"Thank you, Patrick Hart," I manage in a squeaky

voice completely unlike my own. "You're not so bad yourself."

He laughs out loud now, and I'm not sure what to make of it.

"Here," he says as he reaches to give my phone back. "Let me guess. You were going to message Clara and Ella to tell them about me. The Romantics, still together after all these years."

"Well …" I stammer.

If I admit the truth, it will go to his head.

"You'll say nothing but good things, of course," Patrick adds, looking smug. Or maybe it's my imagination, and he isn't looking smug at all. Smug seems to be burned into my memory where Patrick is concerned.

"I don't know," I reply. "You wish."

His hand brushes mine as I grab for the phone. We let our touch linger.

Oh. My. God. What is happening here?

I pull away, then lean sideways onto the project table, one hip jutting out … dare I say, seductively? Patrick's gaze follows. I simultaneously want to throat punch him and kiss him. I wonder if he feels the same way. And I wonder just what in the hell I'm supposed to do about it.

"I do wish," he confirms.

I blush. There's nothing reflective in front of me I can look at to confirm, but I feel fifteen shades of red.

Before I know it, Rachael is at my side. She probably wonders if I need to be bailed out. She's never seen me like this. Hell, I've never seen myself like this either.

Sure, I was somewhat inept at flirting when I met Jay

the other day. And sure, Jay's good looks inspired me to take time for a little self love. But dare I say, this feels … completely different.

I'm not sure how to assess all of that, honestly. I'm not sure I should try. I tell myself to focus on the man who is here now.

"Rosalie," Rachael begins, looking skeptically at Patrick. "Can I help with anything?"

Patrick doesn't take his sexy blue eyes off of me. His gaze is penetrating. And suddenly every word I think sounds sexual. I wonder what else of his could be penetrating. It's juvenile. And I can't seem to help it. A fresh rush of blood makes its way to my pleasure petals.

"Oh, um …" I mumble. I clear my throat nervously as I answer Rachael. "I'm okay."

"You sure about that?" she asks.

She knows me all too well. It wasn't long ago that Rachael commiserated with me at a Christmas party about the horrors of being single during the holidays.

While I admit copious amounts of wine were involved, I spoke from the heart. I proclaimed myself ready to meet the right guy this year. And I meant it. I told Rachael I wasn't looking for a fairy tale romance, but rather a solid companion who would be there for me. Someone who would appreciate me for the good and bad. Someone who could join me as we take it from here together. She insisted that romance should be involved, and I agreed. But she knew what I meant.

I want the real stuff. The nitty gritty, in the trenches, ride or die type of love. I deserve as much.

My job as a florist means I'm dressed up and in

fancy places much of the time. It's lovely—don't get me wrong. But it gives me an appreciation for what happens behind the scenes. I want a love that is beautiful on more than just the outside.

"We're old friends," Patrick explains, jostling me out of my daydream. "Reunited after many years. I don't think Rosalie expected to run into me like this."

He still doesn't take his eyes off of me. He's speaking to Rachael, but he isn't looking at her. It's making me nervous. But it's also making me feel good. Really good. Warm and gooey good.

"You can say that again," I whisper as I open my eyes wide and part my lips. "You are the last person I expected to walk into my shop. You're lucky I don't boot you right out of here, given our history."

Rachael looks concerned now, raising one hand to her chin thoughtfully. "Detailed history?" she asks. "The kind I should know about?"

She's heard enough to get the gist. Now, she's just fishing—probably to get his version of things.

Patrick smirks, and the urge to punch him comes surging back.

"Patrick here was my ... I don't know. Is *nemesis* the right word?" I wink at him, somehow collecting myself and regaining a measure of composure. Maybe it's the adrenaline, at the ready as I consider violence.

He laughs heartily now, enjoying this. I give in and a smile makes its way across my face. It's a small concession. It doesn't mean anything. Yet.

How did he get to be so hot? He's like catnip to a cat, or ... I don't know. Something completely and utterly irresistible to me. It isn't just his looks, either. He has an allure that makes him seem like a nice person and a worthy life partner.

He's probably like a Greek God in bed. Or one of those Magic Mike dancers who can melt your panties in the span of one flaming-hot minute. Cue the Pony song!

Whoo-wee.

I tell myself not to get carried away.

"Say," Patrick suggests, looking at his smartwatch and gesturing towards me. "There's a get-together next Friday at my firm. Nothing too fancy, but we're cele-brating as we kick off the new project."

"Our new project?"

"This building, yeah," he clarifies. "Why don't you join us? Invite Ella and Clara." I look at Rachael. "She's welcome to come along, too." Patrick adds. He still doesn't take his eyes off of me. It would be rude, except that I'm basking in the glow of his attention. I could forgive almost any social faux pas right now.

I may be smitten. Except that I still hate him.

Damn. And now I sound like a broken record. Around and around.

"I don't mean to be a wet blanket here," Rachael begins. A wet blanket? Interesting choice of words for her. She's in her twenties, but sometimes she sounds like my grandmother. "But Rosalie, don't you already have a thing next Friday night?"

"What?" I ask.

Rachael excuses us and takes me to the side where we can talk privately. "You remember. With Jay, from the coffee stand."

"Oh, yeah," I say.

I had completely forgotten about him when considering my schedule. Not that there's anything wrong with Jay Whatever-His-Last-Name-Is. He seems friendly. And smart. I'm sure we'd have a good time out together.

We've established the fact that I'm attracted to him.

"I don't mean to overstep," Rachael continues. "It's just that Jay is the first guy you've made plans with since … You know. I don't want to see you miss a chance at new love."

Ugh. My insides sink as she refers to … You Know. My ex. Rachael doesn't even have to say his name. Just the thought of Jimmy Carlton and his cheating ways is enough to dampen my spirits. That scoundrel.

And now *I* sound like my grandmother.

"I know," I say. "You're right. Jay seems great, and it's been way too long. I need to keep that date. Patrick here isn't worth canceling for. Hell, I'm not sure Patrick is worth the time I've already spent talking to him. He used to harass me something fierce when we were kids. It was bad."

"Then get rid of him. You did call him your nemesis."

"Okay, I will," I say, standing up straighter.

The logical part of my brain seems certain. I should go out with Jay as planned and get rid of Patrick. My nemesis. Good riddance.

A little voice inside of me tries to protest and to root for Patrick, but I push it away. I just met—err, reunited —with Patrick, while Jay goes all the way back to three days ago. And surely, Patrick hasn't changed. The fact that he makes me weak in the knees is probably due to the childhood trauma I experienced at his hands. If not that, I'm sure there's another reasonable explanation. Right?

Right.

Rachael and I walk back to Patrick, then she reaches out to shake his hand. She's pushy for an assistant. I've always liked that about her. I've told myself she has a strong head on her shoulders and might play a larger role in my business someday. Like when I have a baby and want to take time off. But that's way in the distance. No need to think about it anytime soon. Right?

Right.

Why do I feel so unsure of myself since Patrick walked in?

Speaking of that, I can't help but wonder about the advice Rachael just gave me. Why am I listening to her? She's as single as I am. What does she know about finding love, anyway? Hell, she thought Jimmy was a good guy. It was Clara and Ella who saw him for what he really was. Maybe I should be talking to them about Jay and Patrick and my plans for a date night.

"Mr. Hart, is it?" Rachael asks, her voice firm.

"That's right," Patrick says.

He makes eye contact with Rachael out of respect. She is speaking directly to him, after all. But then he turns and winks at me in a smooth motion. I swoon like Scarlett in *Gone With the Wind.*

Oh, my. Be still my heart.

"Thanks for coming in to deliver the paperwork

related to the renovation," Rachael says. "We appreciate it. If we have any questions, we'll be in touch."

Rachael practically pushes Patrick out the front door before he can object.

I glance out at him through the wall of paned windows, and he looks a little like a lost puppy as he stands there in the rain, his cheeks glistening. Our eyes meet and I take a step towards him, but Rachael stops me with a tug on my elbow.

"Don't."

I should listen to her. I do listen to her.

So, I guess that's that. *Done.*

Or is it?

CHAPTER 8

PATRICK

Why does it feel like I've just been punched in the gut?

Ouch.

I don't know what I expected. It isn't like I thought I'd waltz in, sweep Rosalie off her feet, and live happily ever after. I know it doesn't work like that. Not in real life. That script is straight out of the movies. It's fiction. It doesn't happen. Especially not to guys like me. Guys who behaved badly.

In real life, guys who behaved like I did are shunned. Punished, even. I was a prick. I took out my adolescent frustrations about what was happening in my home life at the time on a poor, innocent girl.

If I can ever make up for what I did—and that's a big if—I know it won't be easy.

I hurry to my car and start the ignition. Fat raindrops land on the windshield, warping my view. As I stare back at the front of Rosalie's flower shop and see my reflection in the glass, I wince. I'm suddenly a little self conscious about driving a Tesla.

Do I seem like a jerk now, as an adult? Am I pretentious? I don't intend to be, but I can't help but wonder how I look through Rosalie's eyes.

Fuck me.

I pick up my phone and dial Brandon. He's waiting to hear how things went. I hate to disappoint him, but I don't have much good news to report.

He answers on the second ring.

"Hey, buddy," Brandon says, cheerfully. "How'd it go?"

I run a hand through my hair as I exhale. "It was brutal," I say. "Like Atlanta rush hour traffic on a Friday afternoon … before a holiday weekend."

"That bad?"

"In a word, yes," I reply. "I feel like such an ass."

Brandon pauses, considering his response. His care during tense situations is one of the things I like most about him. I listen to the rain as I wait. When he finally speaks, it isn't what I expected.

"Is Rosalie still in her shop?"

"Yeah," I say. "Why?"

"Can you go back inside?"

At this, my body tenses. "I suppose I could, but why would I want to? I made a fool out of—"

He cuts me off. "Don't overthink it. In fact, don't think about it at all. Here's what you're going to do."

I wonder about the wisdom in his words, but decide I don't have much to lose. I enjoyed being in Rosalie's presence. I'm happy to spend every moment I possibly can with her. Besides, Brandon has good, healthy relationships. He hasn't met the love of his life yet, but I can trust his judgment. His way of relating to family and friends is real and true. He's been an outstanding friend to me.

"Okay," I say, "but I should tell you—"

He cuts me off, again. "You're going to meet me for lunch at Reggie's in an hour. In the meantime, you're going to have a second conversation with Rosalie. A better conversation than the first."

"Okay," I agree. "I like where this is moving."

"Do you have a reason to go back in?" he asks. "Any reason will do. Did you forget something? Or forget to tell her about something?"

I rack my brain. Nothing comes to mind. Until it does. "Oh! I have something. There was a camera crew in there filming for some TV show. I think I was supposed to sign a release to give them permission to use footage I appeared in. I left in a hurry without talking to the producer about it."

"That's good," Brandon replies, and I can hear the warmth in his voice. He wants this to happen for me. He wants to help. "Use that. Go back inside and say you've returned to sign the release."

"Got it."

He doesn't ask if I'm comfortable having my love story filmed for the world to see. He knows it doesn't matter. Rosalie matters. If a camera crew is part of the package, then so be it. Even if I fail spectacularly and become the laughing stock of TV viewers around the globe, at least I will have taken my shot.

"This time, leave the angst from the past at the door," he says. "I'm sure tensions were high when you and Rosalie first reunited. But that's done now. It's time to begin, in earnest, to make up for how you treated her when you were kids. You must right the ship. The last thing you want is for old hurts to create new ones. Nobody wins when that happens."

"I was just thinking essentially the same thing," I say. "We're on the same page."

"Good," my friend replies. "Go back in there and observe with a humble heart. See Rosalie as she is right now. Look for a way to make her day brighter or lighten her load. What you want is a chance to spend time getting to know her."

A lump forms in the back of my throat and I nearly get choked up. "That's exactly what I want to do."

"Then go do it. Keep it simple," he says. "Observe, be humble, and offer her something meaningful. I'll see you at Reggie's in an hour."

I smile. "You aren't even going to tell me how the interview went? I'm dying to know whether you'll be sticking around these parts full time."

"We'll talk over lunch," Brandon replies. "You've got work to do. Now, go."

We hang up the phone, and I know he's right. He's almost always right, but I won't tell him that and let it go to his head.

I take a deep breath and gather my resolve.

I can do this. Keep it simple, stupid.

I'm tempted to ruminate over what to say and not to

say once I get in there, but decide that won't do me a lick of good. I've spent months working up the courage to approach Rosalie. I suspect this is the kind of prize that can only be won by getting into the arena and getting dirty. I might make an even bigger twit of myself. But I have to try.

Yep. I'm doing this.

I go through a repeat of the motions I made a short while ago—exiting the car, dashing through the rain, and opening the door to the flower shop. A bell rings to announce my arrival. When Rosalie—and her assistant, and the cameras, and the crew—turn to face me, I freeze like a deer in headlights on a foggy night. My mouth goes as dry as cotton.

"Patrick?" Rosalie asks.

I like the way my name sounds on her lips.

I clear my throat. "Um, yeah," I mumble. "I'm back."

I can't be certain, but I think I see a hint of a smile. "What for?" she asks.

I lower my brow and raise my shoulders. I'm trying to look nonchalant, but I doubt it's working.

Get this moving, Patch.

My mom calls me Patch. Funny enough, I call myself the nickname when it's time for a pep talk.

"Did you forget something?" Rosalie's assistant asks. I'm pretty sure her name is Rachael.

I turn my attention toward her. Even though I'd rather keep my eyes on Rosalie, I realize that I'll need to get to know her friends, too. Anyone who is important to Rosalie is also important to me. I might as well begin with Rachael.

"Actually, I did," I say with what I hope is a friendly smile. "I think I was supposed to sign a release."

She looks at me blankly, then shrugs.

"For being on camera. I mean, to give my permission to be on camera," I explain. "So they can use the footage filmed while I was here."

"Yeah, that would be helpful," an older man says as he surfaces from a crowd of production people in the back of the room. He's clean cut, and in good shape for his age. He seems like a good dude.

I can usually tell about a man's energy. The bad guys can typically be spotted a mile away.

"I'll sign," I say.

He walks toward me with a manilla file folder in one hand. It's a little grungy around the edges, but I suppose that doesn't matter. We're on location, not in a pristine office space.

"Sonny Hoover," he says as he takes a single sheet of paper out and slides it to me. "I'm the producer."

"Patrick Hart," I say as I take the form and scribble my signature on it. "Although, you probably already know that. I guess you heard our conversation earlier."

I glance at Rosalie sheepishly. She meets my gaze, and it feels like we have an inside secret. Maybe one day, our shared history can be a positive instead of a negative. Granted, I'm clueless as to how that might happen.

Sonny takes the signed release form and returns it to the folder, then shakes my hand. His grip is strong and firm. I like that about him, too.

"I might've heard your name," he says with a chuckle.

"When you said it. And when they did. Repeatedly." He gestures toward Rosalie and Rachael. "You're not exactly the most popular guy around here, at the moment."

"Yeah, I gathered that much," I reply.

"But hey," he says, "the fireworks surrounding your arrival aren't the most notable thing that's happened since we began filming on Monday. If it makes you feel any better."

I laugh, because I'm nervous. I want to ask questions. I know I shouldn't though. It's important that I take this seriously.

I swipe a hand over my mouth, physically wiping the smile off my face.

When Sonny's sure I don't have anything else to add, he gives me a manly nod then disappears into the back of the room again. "Keep rolling," he says to his guys. They do, and I can feel the cameras on me.

It's fine. This is fine.

"Patrick, is that all you needed?" Rachael asks. Her tone is cold.

She's protective of Rosalie. I completely understand. I'd be protective of my friend, too, if I were in Rachael's position. Lord only knows what Rosalie told her about me. Right now, though, Rachael is the gatekeeper. I have to figure out a way to break through her defenses. I need to get on her good side.

"Um, yeah, I guess," I say, and I turn half-way toward the door. Then I hear Brandon's voice in my head, and I stop. "Scratch that. There's something else," I say.

I meet Rosalie's gaze again. She seems … intrigued. This is good.

"What?" Rosalie asks.

"Yeah, what?" Rachael parrots.

Think fast, Patch. Come up with something. Anything.

I glance around the room, searching. My gaze lands on the broken vase of gardenias that's still on the floor. I could offer to help clean it up. That's too cliche, though. Isn't it? This isn't a rom-com movie. No one is going to break into song and dance while we sweep flower petals into a dustpan.

"Um," I stammer.

"Mr. Hart, will that be all?" Rachael asks.

She's growing impatient with me. I don't blame her.

"It's … well …"

I look at Rosalie, my eyes pleading. I want an excuse to spend more time with her. When she smiles and nods, it gives me the inspiration I need.

"It's about the renovation," I blurt, satisfied.

"Yes?" Rosalie asks.

"Yes," I reply. "There are some details we really should go over."

"I will probably have questions," she says. But just as fast, she seems to develop second thoughts. "Oh, nevermind. I'm sure the answers are in the materials you gave me earlier."

"It won't take long," I say, and I hope I don't sound desperate. "I could swing by this evening after the shop is closed. Around 6, maybe? I can explain everything then."

No one in the room is sure whether I'm referring to

the renovation details or why I acted like such an idiot when we were kids. I'm not certain, myself.

Rachael crosses her arms over her chest and rolls her eyes.

Rosalie appears unsure, but she isn't saying no.

A heavy silence falls over us. We look back and forth at each other for a long minute until, finally, good ol' Sonny provides an assist.

I knew I liked that guy.

"I'd love to capture your discussion on film," Sonny says. "The renovation will be a big part of this docuseries. It makes sense to get some early footage of the two of you going over plans."

I practically jump with joy. "Understood," I say. "I'm happy to help. And you already have my signed release. Six o'clock?"

"Six works well for me," Sonny replies. "Rosalie? Can you make that happen?"

She nods and laughs, a huge grin spreading across her face. "Yes, I can make that happen," she says.

I think she forgot to hate me, if only for a moment.

"Six, it is."

CHAPTER 9

PATRICK

"Score board," I say as I slide into a chair across from Brandon. "Boo-ya!"

"Yeah?" he asks, a slow smile forming.

I place both palms on the table like an underdog coach who's down for the count, but who believes he might actually have a shot at winning the game.

"You're looking at a man who will be in the company of one Ms. Rosalie Flowers at six o'clock this evening," I announce.

"No way!" Brandon says.

"Yes, way," I reply.

"See! I told you. Where there's a will, there's a way," he muses. "How did you do it? What's happening at six?"

A waiter arrives to take our drink order. My enthusiasm must be contagious, because he gives me a high-five. We chat for a few minutes about my interest in getting the girl. When we've all agreed that a good woman is worth the chase, he excuses himself and returns to the kitchen.

"At six, I'm heading back to the flower shop to go over reno paperwork," I explain.

"Simple and easy," Brandon says.

"Easier than I expected," I agree. "I told Rosalie I thought there were some things we should discuss. She hesitated, but the producer of the TV show that's being filmed stepped up as my wingman. Can you believe that?"

He smiles big, as if he knows that my story will have a happy ending. "I definitely can," he says. "When things are meant to be, they have a way of working themselves out."

I laugh out loud, nervously. "Hey, now," I say as the waiter sets two glasses of sweet tea in front of us. "Don't jinx it."

The waiter pauses, listening to us. It seems like he wants to get in on the conversation. Brandon and I don't mind chatting. It's what people do in a small, Southern town. It's kind of nice. Waiters in Buckhead aren't always as friendly.

"Jinx what?" the guy asks.

I glance at his name tag. It reads Rod. He's young. Maybe college age, although I doubt he's in college if he's working here in Loveland at lunch time. The nearest large universities are Vanderbilt, Belmont, and Tennessee State University in Nashville. There's also Middle Tennessee State in Murfreesboro. They're all thirty to forty-five minutes away. I don't know, though.

Maybe Rod attends classes online. Virtual learning seems to be all the rage these days.

It's remarkable how much things have changed since I was in college a decade ago. The pandemic is to blame for a lot of it, I'm sure. I wonder how it will be by the time I have a kid of my own in college.

Okay, wow. Hold your horses there, Patch. Where did that even come from?

I refocus and shoot Brandon a look. If we're going to be living here, I suppose we should get to know the locals. He nods his approval, so I tell Rod more of my story.

"Whoa," Rod replies. He folds his round serving tray flat against his abdomen as he ponders the magnitude of my quest. He's wearing a white shirt under a black apron. It's somewhat formal, until you see his jeans and tennis shoes on the bottom half. "What are the odds?" he asks.

"That she'll agree to date me?" I ask.

"No, that you'd be obsessed with a girl you teased in middle school."

I recoil a bit. I'm offended by the word obsessed. "I'm not sure I'd describe it that way," I say. "It sounds so creepy when you say it like that. It's not like I'm stalking her or anything. I'm not following her around town, or standing outside her condo in the dark."

"But you know she lives in a condo and not a house?" Rod asks jokingly.

I shake my head, deciding how to take this guy.

Brandon narrows one eye and gives me a sympathetic look. "It's all in the way you frame it, my friend," he says.

"I'm sorry," Rod adds. "I don't want to butt in. It's just that it's crazy to think about what you're trying to do. You have to admit that. How mean were you? As a kid?"

I lean back in my chair and raise a hand to my chin. When I do, Rod seems to take it as an invitation. He pulls out a chair and sits with us, glancing back toward the kitchen long enough to make sure no one is looking for him.

I guess we're doing this.

I showed up here expecting a chat with Brandon, alone. But hey, I might as well go with the flow. Right? Maybe this kid will have something insightful to share.

"I'm not sure," I say. "We were children. I had issues at home. My parents fought like cats and dogs in the years leading up to their divorce. It was tough for everyone involved. My brother and I had to find a way to cope with all the yelling we were exposed to on a daily basis."

"Wait," Rod says. "You have a brother?"

I nod. "Yep."

"And he knows—or knew—this girl, too?"

"He did."

Rod wrinkles his face so tightly, it looks like he's smelled something foul.

"What's with the face?" I ask.

"Has your brother talked to her? Now that you're all old?" he asks.

Brandon lets a chuckle escape. He's been mostly

listening, but he seems to find this guy as funny as I do. "Son, how old are *you*?"

"Twenty," Rod says. "I'll be twenty-one in a few months. Then I'll be legal to drink and everything." He shrugs. "I can serve alcohol now. And more importantly, I can serve our country in the military. I reckon I should be able to drink legally, too, but that's beside the point. I can't change the law. People smarter than me have tried."

Brandon grunts his agreement. "Uh huh. What makes you think we're so old?"

Rod shrugs, then points to me. "He said boo-ya."

At that, we break into raucous laughter. Something about Rod's comment hits Brandon and me in the funny bones. We feed off each other, laughing so long that tears form in the corners of our eyes.

"Is that all it takes to qualify a person as old?" Brandon asks when he's calmed down enough to breathe. He looks at me as he continues, "Watch out, Patrick. Say 'boo-ya' once and you're over the hill. You had better call for your Medicare insurance plan when you leave here. That is, unless the office staff at your new assisted living facility plan to take care of that for you."

We belly laugh together.

"Yeah, you found me out, Rod," I say. "I'm going to get fitted for my dentures tomorrow."

"Right after your hearing aids?" Brandon adds.

"Oh, those are already at home on top of my dresser. You didn't know? I keep them next to my suspenders and beside my Depends," I say.

"Okay, okay," Rod says. "I get it. You aren't as old as you look. Sorry."

That only sends Brandon and me into more fits of laughter. It's crowded in the restaurant, and people are beginning to notice our noisy discussion.

"And just how old do we look?" I ask.

Rod shrugs again. "I'm not a good judge of these things, obviously. You wouldn't be laughing so hard if I was."

"How about you answer the question?" Brandon says, prodding him. "Enquiring minds want to know."

"What?" Rod asks. "That doesn't make any sense."

Brandon and I share a knowing glance. He's pulling phrases from before our time now. I know the enquiring minds phrase because my dad used to say it. That's how I know the word boo-ya, too. I don't tell Rod any of that, though. I'm enjoying a chance to watch him squirm. It's taking my mind off of my troubles.

"Let's stick to the basics," I say. "How old do you think we are?"

He looks at us hard as he assesses our ages. "My dad's age. I guess. Maybe you're a little younger. You could probably have kids my age. Right?"

"Dude," I say, "I'm not even thirty. To have a kid your age, I would have had to get someone knocked up when I was ten."

"Actually, nine," Brandon adds with a laugh. "Don't forget to figure in time for the pregnancy."

"There you go," I say. "Insemination at age nine. Now that's hilarious."

"I am over thirty," Brandon adds. "Thirty-two, in fact. So yeah, it would have been age twelve for me."

"I told you. I don't know," Rod says, looking embarrassed. "I shouldn't have said anything."

He stands and pulls out his pad and pen to take our order. "What can I get you?"

"We're just kidding around," I say. "Don't take us too seriously."

Rod's shoulders droop and he drops the pad of paper back into his apron pocket. "It's okay," he says. He glances over his shoulder at the kitchen. An older woman behind the register shoots him a dirty look, but he doesn't seem overly concerned.

The mood is more serious now. We didn't intend to hurt the kid's feelings.

"What's up?" Brandon asks him.

"My dad," Rod replies. "He owns the place."

"You're Reggie's boy?" I ask.

"The one and only," he confirms. "I took a semester off from school and am working here to save enough money to get back to Memphis and get my own apartment instead of having to live in those nasty dorms. I don't want to disappoint my dad. I didn't mean any disrespect toward you guys."

"No harm, no foul," I say.

Rod strikes me as a sports guy. He'll get the reference. At least, I think he will. Now, everything I say makes me feel old.

Thanks a lot, kid.

Brandon offers a few words of reassurance, too, and within minutes, Rod seems good as new.

Before we reach the point of giving him our lunch orders, though, an old lady with hair as white as snow walks over to our table. Her eyes are bright. She looks excited, almost like she knows us from somewhere. As she gets closer, I can tell that her attention is focused on me. Maybe she knows me from somewhere. Come to think of it, maybe I recognize her.

"My apologies," she says as she puts a hand on Rod's forearm. "I hate to interrupt, but Patrick Hart, is that you?"

Her voice seals the deal. I definitely know this woman. "Principal Livingston?" I ask.

"Why, yes!" she exclaims. "The one and only. I've been sitting over there," she says as she points to a nearby area of the dining room, "and I thought that was you. I told my husband I had to come over and say hi."

She turns and waves at her husband, who looks like a peaceable man. He smiles and waves back, then returns his attention to a bowl of something. Probably soup.

Rod seems energized by our reunion. He decides to speak freely. Maybe he's young and impulsive, and always speaks freely. Either way, he jumps right in there.

"Principal?" he asks. "As in, his principal?"

"That's right," Mrs. Livingston says.

Rod claps his hands and throws his head back. "High school or middle school? Or elementary school?"

"Middle school," she replies. "Loveland Middle. I was principal there for nearly two decades. Patrick and his little brother were my students."

I squirm a little, suddenly feeling flush. Principal Livingston knew me during the most difficult years of my life. I acted out—a lot—and she was often the one who ended up disciplining me. I don't necessarily want to revisit that.

"So," Reggie continues with the gusto of a young reporter in pursuit of a hot story, "you knew the girl he picked on?"

Principal Livingston eyes me, her face cautious. "Sure. I know Rosalie. She grew up to be quite a pillar of our fine community, wouldn't you say, Patrick?"

"I would."

I feel like I'm watching a car about to be driven off a cliff. I don't like it and can't stop it. Yet, I can't look away, either.

"Rosalie?" Rod asks. "As in the Rosalie who owns Rosalie's Flowers?"

"That's right," she replies. "Her last name is Flowers. Her shop is *the* cutest. Not to mention, The Romantics wedding services group she heads up is doing some amazing work—and growing by leaps and bounds. From what I've heard, it's bringing all kinds of tourists and newcomers to our little town. We were in desperate need of new life around here."

Rod smirks. Apparently, he knows Rosalie. Or knows of her. He leans toward me and whispers, "you didn't mention that the girl was Rosalie Flowers."

"Does it matter?" I ask.

Brandon is amused, but he isn't saying anything.

"My parents and I know her," Rod says. "That's all. Rosalie used to babysit me sometimes on Saturdays while my dad went fishing and my mom went to play cards with her Nashville friends. I might could put in a good word for you, if you want."

"What's this about?" Principal Livingston asks me. "I thought you moved to Georgia—and stayed. I knew your dad was still here, but I thought you were gone, Patrick."

Why do I feel like I'm about to get a stern lecture? It feels like seventh grade, all over again.

"What are you doing back?" she continues. "And what do you want with Rosalie? I'm sort of surprised you don't plan to leave well enough alone in that regard. You weren't very nice to her. Neither was Jesse."

Great. Now my interest in Rosalie has officially entered into the town gossip mill. That's just what I need. Where's Sonny and his camera crew? Because that would be the icing on the cake right now. Let's hope no one calls them to come on over.

I close my eyes for a beat to gather my thoughts. I remind myself that this will all be worth it in the end. If Rosalie returns my affection, all of the uncomfortable comments and embarrassment will have been one hundred percent worth it.

"You were rude to Rosalie Flowers?" a woman at another nearby table asks.

Fuck me.

"No," I say, feeling cornered. "Well, yes, but not recently. When we were kids—"

"He wants to date her now," Rod announces.

"Thanks for that, Rod," I say.

"Easy," Brandon tells me as he puts a hand on my

shoulder. "These folks are looking out for Rosalie. That's all. She's a beloved member of this community, based on what I've heard."

"She sure is," the random woman at the nearby table says. "Everyone loves Rosalie. She's still grieving after her mom's passing."

"Then there was the nasty breakup," Rod adds.

I react, leaning back hard in my seat.

Principal Livingston smiles, and she holds the room's attention. She has an air about her that commands authority. As a principal should. "You didn't know," she says to me, her tone softening. It's a statement, not a question.

I shake my head. "I had no idea," I say softly. "I remember her mom. She was always nice. She baked the best peanut butter cookies every year at Christmas time and brought them into our class." I look up at Principal Livingston. "What happened to her?"

"Lung cancer," she says, sadly. "She wasn't even a smoker."

"Oof," I say with a soft moan. "Damn."

"Eight months ago," Rod adds. "I remember the date because I skipped basketball practice one day to come home for the funeral." His tone has changed, too.

I shake my head. I wish this wasn't true. I hate the thought of Rosalie being hurt. It makes me wish I could fight on her behalf, only there's no one to fight. My thoughts move on to the rest.

"The breakup?" I ask. "What's the story there?"

The lady at the nearby table opens her mouth to speak, but Principal Livingston raises a finger to stop her. "That story isn't one for us to share," she says. "We don't know the intimate details, anyway. If Rosalie decides she wants you to know, she'll tell you herself. Suffice to say, our Rosie has had a tough year."

I smile, hearing her nickname. "Rosie? Is that what her friends call her?"

Principal Livingston nods.

"So do the kids she babysat," Rod adds. "It fits, what with her rosy personality."

I look at Brandon as I take it all in. He nods again, apparently in no hurry, so I invite Principal Livingston and her husband to sit with us. Maybe it's nice, living in a small town and running into people you used to know. That never happened to me in Atlanta.

We enjoy a delicious, slow meal with good conversation and even better company. Rod sits with us periodically, when he has a few minutes to spare. He also introduces us to his dad, Reggie, who is a well-loved local treasure.

By the time we're finished with lunch, I have a full belly and an entirely different perspective on my world.

CHAPTER 10

ROSALIE

"Holy moley!" I say to Clara when she answers the phone. I'm sitting at my desk. "You *have* to hear what happened to me today."

If I was talking to Ella, I would use more colorful language.

"Oohh, is it something good?" Clara asks. "Because you know I love good news."

"I don't know," I reply, although my voice gives me away.

Of course, it's something good. I think. Dammit.

"Then tell me!"

I turn and slump behind a big bundle of baby's breath so Rachael doesn't see me, then I exhale deeply. And I smile.

"I will," I promise. "But Ella needs to hear this, too. Our spot in fifteen?"

"I'll be there."

"And tell El I have important news, would you? I called you first."

"Done!" Clara replies, excited with me.

I hang up the phone and pump my fist in the air like a freak. I'm not sure if Rachael notices. Now, to do a little internet digging.

"Rachael, dear?" I call out across the studio, straightening up in my chair.

No clients are here, so I can get away with it. I only have to make sure my voice carries over Eric Clapton playing in the background. We keep love songs on, and *Wonderful Tonight* is a favorite.

I'd like a man to sing to me about how wonderful I look.

I wonder if Patrick has a good singing voice. His speaking voice makes me think he probably does. It's so warm and lush, like a toasty fire on a cold night. I wonder what it sounds like during intimate moments. I'm guessing that man could melt me into a puddle on the floor if he were to whisper sweet nothings into my ear.

"Yes?" Rachael answers, poking her head out from the supply closet.

She's preparing to clean up the gardenias I knocked over. She's a doll. Maybe I'm becoming my grandmother, calling my assistant a doll. Maybe that's why Rachael and I get along so well together. Deep down, we're a couple of old ladies. Maybe I should embrace it.

"I have some computer work to do, and then I'm going out for a while. Will you watch the shop and answer the phone?"

I act as if she could say no. She is my employee. She has to do what I ask.

"Sure thing," she calls back. "Should we pretend your computer work doesn't involve googling Patrick?"

"We should."

"Fine," she chirps.

I'm sure she's amused by all of this. I don't blame her.

"Fine," I reply.

Sonny and his crew are still here, of course, but I'm taking his imperative seriously. I'm getting skilled at ignoring their presence altogether.

I pop open my laptop, launch my web browser, and type Patrick's name into the search bar. I don't have long before I'll need to head out to meet Clara and Ella. I had better be efficient. Luckily, Patrick's name returns a slew of results. His life appears to be well documented on the web.

The first result is a website for his Loveland-based firm, Hart Design+Build. It looks all polished and professional. White letters over top of an image of a particularly gorgeous interior space tell me that it's an integrated architecture, design, engineering, construction, and interior design outfit. Apparently, Patrick and his associates are a one-stop shop of sorts when it comes to renovations and new builds. I find that fact strangely alluring. Pretty houses are a not-so-secret passion of mine. I love everything about them.

I live in a cozy condo above a bakery on Second Street, just me and my tabby cat named Tabatha. I love living there, with its bustling downtown charm and sweet aromas wafting up through the rafters. But it's long been a dream of mine to buy and renovate an old farmhouse on a few acres of land. In fact, there are properties on the outskirts of town I've been stalking for months now. Money isn't the issue. Business has been good and I have the savings. What I don't have is the experience and the manpower to be sure the renovation is done right.

Sounds like Patrick and his crew could make my dream a reality. I can imagine it now … Me picking out tile and countertops while gently patting my pregnant belly with one hand and the top of Tabatha's little head with the other. Patrick would, of course, look sexy in a hardhat as he walks the property and checks on the project's progress. I'd try not to fall on my ass like I did the day we met—err, reunited.

Stop it, Rosalie. You sound ridiculous. You don't know this guy. The only thing you know for sure is how horrible he treated you when you were kids. Stop. It.

And now I'm talking to myself at length. At least, I'm doing it silently. It would be a lot worse if I were doing it out loud.

As I click around the firm's website, I practically drool over the before and after pictures. These folks clearly know what they're doing, and they have impeccable taste. One page notes awards they've won, while another features testimonials from happy clients. I'm officially impressed.

I can't help but wonder how I missed this. The website makes it look like Patrick has been operating in Loveland for a while now. And I had no idea he was here. He hadn't even crossed my mind. It's a fairly small town. People know each other. Maybe I've just been too preoccupied with my own issues to lift my head up and look around. It's pretty much all flowers all the time in my world. Well, mostly.

I navigate to the About Us page. It features Patrick's handsome face at the top, along with two other guys who look like they could be related to him. All three of them share the same strong jawline and piercing eyes. They look like movie stars. Or superheroes.

Wait a minute ... These guys *are* related to Patrick. The captions below list one Richard Hart and ... *Oh, no. What in the actual hell?*

This can't be true. Just my luck.

Next to Patrick's profile is a photo of Jay. The very same Jay from the coffee stand. The very same Jay I have a date with next Friday. And the very same Jay who isn't actually just Jay at all, but JT.

I must not have been paying close attention when he told me his name. It was loud. Maybe he said JT and I only heard the beginning. No matter, there it is in front of me, spelled out plainly. He's JT Hart, as in Jesse Hart.

Things just got super complicated.

How could I have missed this? I guess I shouldn't be too hard on myself. Jesse looks completely different than he did when we were kids. He is two years younger than the rest of us. He hadn't even hit puberty when they moved to the city.

I must say, the years have been kind to Jesse ... or JT, as he apparently wants to be called. He's as handsome as they come. Tall like his brother, and with the same thick, dark hair and intense eyes. Come to think of it, Patrick and Jesse—it feels weird to call him JT—must get their good looks from their dad. If I were thirty years older, I'd be all about Richard Hart just like I am his sons.

There. I said it. I'm interested in both Jesse and Patrick. It's absurd. But there it is.

My love life has been practically nonexistent ever since last fall when I found out that Jimmy was cheating on me. He broke my heart to pieces. I had fancied myself the future Mrs. Carlton. I had a gown from Ella's bridal shop picked out ... even though Jimmy never said he wanted to marry me.

There were warning signs I should have picked up on. I fully admit I let my guard down and trusted the wrong man. In the back of my mind, I knew something wasn't right. But I allowed myself to dream. I had wanted us to have it all, together.

Jimmy is a morning radio host based in Nashville. For a long time, he commuted into the city at an ungodly hour every weekday. He's kind of a local celebrity— Loveland's own, like Patrick called me. I like the phrase better coming out of Patrick's pretty mouth, that's for sure.

Jimmy's not even from Tennessee, but when he got the job in Nashville, he decided to settle here in Loveland and commute. He said small-town life reminded him of his hometown in rural Texas. He claimed he'd rather live in a place with picturesque views than a high-rise building in a concrete jungle. I didn't blame him. But I should have trusted my instincts and been wary.

Maybe I was starstruck. I don't like to think of myself as a person who could become starstruck.

I'm aware that celebrities are people just like the rest of us. But there was something about Jimmy being from rural Texas and then becoming widely known as a result of his job on the radio that made him especially appealing. It was as if I got some fresh catch before the other ladies of Loveland had a chance to snag him for themselves. He was all mine. Or so I thought.

Jimmy is tall and looks remarkably like Patrick and Jesse. In fact, he could be a cousin of theirs. If I didn't know better, I'd suspect that maybe he was related. I guess I have a type. Ah, well. Don't we all?

My relationship with Jimmy was good for a while. But it wasn't long until he claimed commuting was too much every day. He leased an apartment in the city and only came home to his cottage here in Loveland on weekends.

At first, he assured me I was welcome to join him in the city anytime. And I did, when my schedule allowed. Some of the best sex of my life was with Jimmy in his Downtown Nashville apartment as the city lights twinkled outside. He was an attentive and sensual lover. My body warms remembering just how much so.

Our lovemaking sessions always started the same way. He'd rest his hands on top of my shoulders with the pads of his thumbs at the nape of my neck. I got so used to the routine that just feeling his hands there made me wild with desire.

I had to be patient. He'd begin by massaging my shoulders in a slow and deliberate motion that sent shivers down to my toes. Heat radiated off his hands. As my muscles relaxed, Jimmy would bend forward and lean his head gently on the back of mine. It was a sweet posture. It anchored us together as our hands explored each other's bodies and made each other feel good.

Slowly, he'd move his palms down to the small of my back and wrap them firmly around my waist, massaging me along the way. By the time he slid a finger under my bra or between my legs, I was completely at his mercy. I would have done anything for that man.

So, when I found out *my* Jimmy had another girlfriend in the city, I was devastated.

I spent the following week hiding in my condo, scarcely washing my hair or changing my pajamas. I watched sappy romantic comedies on repeat and helped myself to carton after carton of ice cream. I didn't bother with a bowl, but instead brought the entire container with me to the couch. I dug into it as if it would somehow save my life. I didn't even care if the sweet goo melted on my lap before I could polish it all off. I shoveled spoonful after spoonful in until finally, Clara and Ella came over and told me enough was enough.

I think even Tabatha was sick of my wallowing at that point. She'd nudge me with one of her soft paws as if she was trying to pry me off the couch. It was pathetic.

I was pathetic.

Looking back, mama's death the month before probably didn't help matters. Maybe I would have been in a different frame of mind if I hadn't been tangled in grief.

I suppose there's no good time to go through a bad breakup. But that had to have been the worst. It was a one-two punch that nearly knocked me all the way out.

"You'd better get going," Rachael says, snapping me back to reality. "You don't want to keep your friends waiting."

Rachael is in front of me now, her mousy brown hair dancing as the breeze from the overhead air toys with it. Her white blouse is as pristine as the gardenias. She looks every bit the picture of a perky springtime flower shop assistant. She's good for business.

"Right," I say, closing the lid to my laptop and standing up. "On my way. Thanks for watching the shop."

"It's my job," she replies sweetly. "Like, literally."

"I realize that. But I want you to know how much I appreciate you."

She narrows her eyes. She knows me.

"Does that mean you'll be out all afternoon?" she asks.

I smile. I've just hatched a plan.

"Maybe."

"Good for you," she says. "I'll take care of things here."

"Even the gardenias?"

"Even the gardenias."

CHAPTER 11

ROSALIE

As I climb the stairs to our spot, I can hear Clara and Ella laughing and talking together.

Ever since we bought the building a few years ago, we've been meeting here in this dusty old room that probably used to be an office for a factory foreman. We cleaned it up just enough to house a simple table and chairs. There's no decor other than the walls of windows on three sides. I'll bet it's going to be nice after the renovation.

Sonny and two additional cameramen follow me like baby ducks behind a mama. I tried to talk them out of it. They insisted.

"Hey, hey, ladies," I say as I open the door. "How you doin'?"

I try my best to sound like Joey Tribbiani from *Friends*. It's a running joke from our childhood. It's how we greet each other when no one else is around. Or in this case, when we're pretending no one else is around.

"Rosie!" Clara says, her excited voice even louder than it was on the phone.

She and Ella rush towards me and wrap their arms tightly around my neck. It's also how we greet each other when no one else is around.

"Good news, eh?" Ella says. "Clara told me there's something you done. What is it?"

She sounds remarkably like a Long Island mobster. I'm pretty sure she has an uncle or two involved in the real thing. She tones it down when she's talking to clients at her bridal shop, but the attitude is there, never far from the surface. I find her a bundle of contradictions. It's hilarious and adorable.

"Not so much something I've done … yet," I reply with a wink. "Maybe *someone* I might want to do. Maybe more than one someone."

Both ladies squeal now like we're at a Las Vegas bachelorette party. If they had sequins or confetti, they'd be throwing it at me.

"Tell us everything!" Clara sings. "Sounds juicy."

"About damn time," Ella adds. "Brush the cobwebs out of the party palace before they take up permanent residence."

I chuckle, but mostly ignore that snarky remark. Ella's in the middle of a dry spell of her own. I could say the same to her. But that's beside the point.

I sit in a wooden chair and kick my feet up on the farm table as I prepare to begin. I lace my hands behind my head and lean back. It's a masculine pose that might not seem proper for a female owner of a flower shop. But I can be completely at ease with these two.

"Well, go ahead with whatever it is," Clara prompts. "We're listening."

She's, truly, the most straight-laced of the three of us. She owns a travel agency, but has never been on a plane. Can you believe that? She's a small town girl through and through. We need to get her out on an adventure one day soon. It's long overdue.

"You'll never guess who walked into my shop a while ago…" I begin. "Never in a hundred million years."

They look at each other quizzically, wondering if the other has any clue.

"Who?" Ella asks.

"No guesses?" I try.

I don't want it to be too easy. I figure they should work for it a little. I enjoy watching them speculate.

"I don't want to dampen the mood," Clara says. "But was it Jimmy?"

"Stop it," Ella scolds as she swipes Clara on the shoulder.

It's okay. I was already thinking about Jimmy. I'm not upset that Clara mentioned him.

"No," I say sternly. "No time for that noise."

"Sorry," Clara replies. "I didn't mean—"

"Moving on," Ella says. She takes a deep breath, then lets a relaxed smile settle over her face.

I grin at my friends.

"Oh!" Clara starts again. "Jay from the coffee stand?"

"She already has a date with him," Ella says. "Right, Rosalie? Next Friday night? Although, I'm not sure why you didn't make plans with him sooner. Why the long wait?"

It suddenly strikes me that if we bring Rachael into the fold, we could be the new Golden Girls. Ella would be our Sophia. No question. Clara would have to be our Rose. Which would make me ... Dorothy? Blanche? That's a toss up. Rachael and I would have to fight over the remaining role.

And again, I sound like my grandmother. I should probably embrace it. There are worse people I could be compared to.

"You're right. I do have a date with the guy from the coffee stand," I confirm, choosing my words carefully. "You already know that. You two had front row seats to the spectacle, in all of its revealing glory. I just hope our TV show doesn't turn out more like the Kardashian's than the chef from North Carolina's."

They giggle and nod.

"But you said two ..." Ella prompts.

"That's right. Two handsome men have my heart aflutter."

"Rosie!" Clara chirps again.

"And the craziest part is that we all know them. Both of them."

My friends look at each other in disbelief.

"Wait. What?" Clara asks. "I don't know a Jay around here. I'm sure of it."

Ella raises her eyebrows as she gives me her best skeptical face. I bite my lip to keep from grinning from ear to ear. I quite like my little love triangle. At least, I do for the moment. I'm well aware that it will soon become troublesome. All love triangles do.

"Spit it out already!" Ella exclaims, leaning forward and hammering a closed fist down on the table.

If I didn't know her so well, I might find her scary. Her long styled hair, elegant clothing, and perfectly painted face are merely a facade. Ella Lovelace is tough as nails.

"Fine," I say.

I take a deep breath and close my eyes, savoring my secret a moment longer before it leaves my lips.

"You remember Patrick Hart, right?"

"That little pissant who tortured you in school?" Ella asks without skipping a beat.

"That's the one."

"I always did want to thump him," she adds. "Should've done it. The prick."

I laugh at my friend's protectiveness. It's sweet. Clara nods her agreement.

"Then I trust you also remember his brother, Jesse?"

"Sure. He was a grade behind us, right?" Clara asks.

"Two, actually."

"So, what?" Ella blurts, growing more impatient.

I smile bigger. I can't help it. I feel like the belle of the ball. Thanks to the Hart brothers, my body has warmed with desire after a long cold snap. I wasn't sure it would happen for me again. I'm all stirred up in all the right places.

"So, Patrick showed up at my flower shop a little while ago. He's dreamy."

I say it in a whisper. Like I'm telling a secret. Because I am.

A whirring noise sounds as one of the cameras zooms in.

"What?" Clara ponders. "But how? I thought they moved to Georgia. With their mom. Didn't their parents get a divorce? I seem to remember rumors of a nasty split. My mom has always been a sucker for town gossip, and that story kept her busy for weeks."

"They did," I confirm. "The boys are back. Working with their dad at his design+build firm."

Clara raises one hand to her face and furrows her brow, then relaxes as she realizes.

"Ah, Hart Design+Build. I should have made that connection. But, why was Patrick at your flower shop?"

"Because their firm is remodeling the building. We hired them," I explain.

"Actually, Clara," Ella inserts with a chuckle. "*You* hired them. This is all your fault."

It's what we get for letting the ditziest one of us make hiring decisions. Maybe we can blame it on Matt Sellinger, Clara's group sales guy. He does general business management stuff, too. And he's fairly new. Clara hired him a few months ago to help out with an uptick in the number of destination weddings her company makes travel arrangements for. I can see him being the missing link in this situation.

"Damn. I'm sorry," Clara says with a sigh. "But in my defense, Matt is the one who met with the Harts. I reviewed the documents and talked to Richard Hart on the phone. I never met with any of them in person. They came so highly recommended that I didn't think I needed to. And the connection never occurred to me. I haven't thought about Patrick or Jesse for ages."

"I get that," I affirm. "No big deal. If anything, it's kind of funny. Isn't it?"

"Oh, it's definitely funny," Clara laughs. "Patrick Hart has your heart aflutter. Well, well, well. Of all people!"

"I know," I say. "But I also still hate him. Like Ella said … the prick."

"What does this have to do with Jay from the coffee stand?" Ella asks, keeping us focused on the matter at hand.

I swing my legs down and sit up straight for emphasis. This is where the plot thickens.

"That's the craziest part. I did some googling, and it turns out that Jay from the coffee stand isn't just Jay."

"What?" Clara asks eagerly.

"What does that mean?" Ella echoes. "He isn't just Jay? Isn't that his name?"

"When I looked at the bios on the Hart Design+Build website, there was a picture of Jay from the coffee stand right next to Patrick. Jay apparently goes by JT now … and he's actually Jesse Hart himself! Can you believe it?"

"Rosie!" Clara squeals as she stands up and jumps around. "You like them both? And they both like *you*?"

I squint my eyes, bracing for the inevitable razzing to come.

"I guess. Yeah, I guess I do."

Ella claps her hands and stands to join Clara in a

little happy dance. They pull me up with them and hug me as we bounce with excitement.

We pipe love songs throughout the whole building, and Al Green's "Let's Stay Together" is playing as we celebrate. It's sweet, although probably premature.

"Oh, Rosie," Clara coos as she pats my arm. "This has to be a sign. You just said at Christmas how you were ready to meet *the one* this year. And now, the Hart brothers have returned to your life in the most unexpected way. It can't be an accident."

"I don't know," I say. "Let's not forget that I hate them. Especially Patrick. He was terrible to me."

They both stop bouncing and eye me carefully.

"We were kids," Ella says.

"And just a few minutes ago, you were ready to thump him," I add.

"Maybe I'll let him off the hook. If you like him, I mean. He might've changed."

I take a deep breath and close my eyes again. I feel like I'm in a romantic movie, at the part where the guarded and jaded girl decides it's okay to dream big. There's always that part. It's a turning point. Regardless of what happens afterward, she's forever changed by having opened herself up. Only she typically has just one man in her sights.

"Maybe," I agree.

We stand quietly for a moment, taking it all in. Sonny and his camera guys are quiet as well. You could hear a pin drop.

"Rosie, hun," Ella inquires as gently as she can in her

Long-Island-mobster voice. "What are you going to do?"

I smile. Because I have a plan.

"Good question. I'll go out with Jesse as scheduled. He asked first."

"You mean ... Patrick asked you out too?" Clara says.

"Sort of. For next Friday night. Rachael jumped in and reminded me that I had a previous commitment. Of course, Patrick had no idea it was with his brother."

"Naughty girl," Clara teases.

"I said no to next Friday, but Patrick is coming by at six o'clock this evening to go over some things related to the reno. Sonny here said it would be helpful if they could film the discussion."

I glance at Sonny and wink. He might have thought he was helping Patrick, but I want him to know he was actually helping the both of us. I want him to know that I approve of his tactics.

"Is it just me, or is it getting hot in here?" Ella asks with a wink.

"It isn't just you," I say, winking back. "I'm good and ready to turn up the heat. In fact, I'm taking the rest of the afternoon off to go shopping for a few killer outfits. Maybe a manicure and some tidying up, if you know what I mean. Now that I know who Jay from the coffee stand is, I want to be sure I'm, shall we say, *ready* for anything over the next few weeks."

"Good plan," Clara says. "Where is Jesse taking you?"

"I don't even know. I guess it'll be a surprise. We have more than a week between now and then to decide."

"And Patrick?" Ella asks. "I'm sure you'll end up going somewhere other than your flower shop to *discuss the renovation.*" She uses air quotes for emphasis. "Maybe not today. Maybe not even tomorrow. But one day soon, you'll be on a real date with him. Yes?"

"He'll have to wait his turn."

My friends jump and squeal again. They're enjoying this.

"That's right," Ella says. "Make him wait. One at a time until you choose. Single file, boys."

We laugh heartily together. It feels good. These are my closest friends. Really, they're more like sisters. Someday, when I get married, they'll be there by my side for every minute. And not just to provide a gown and travel arrangements. It brings a tear to my eye just thinking about it.

"I love you two," I say. "You do know that, right?"

"We do," Ella says, smiling.

"Of course, we do," Clara confirms.

We hug each other tightly, basking in the glow of my happy news.

"Either of you want to come with me?" I ask.

I know it's a long shot. We all have business to tend to.

"Nah," Ella says. "I'm prepping dresses for the Chestnut Hill Lodge affair happening on Saturday. No time."

"And I'm up to my elbows in paperwork as I continue to train Matt in his new role," Clara replies. "It would be fun. But duty calls."

Before I can protest and try to convince them to join

me, Ella has moved on to a wild new idea. "Hey, why don't you invite one of your boys to attend the wedding with you on Saturday? I'll be there to run interference, if necessary."

I scoff. "I'll be busy wrangling flower arrangements," I say. "You know how it is."

"Who better than a strapping Hart brother to help you with the heavy lifting?" she asks.

"Rosie," Clara says, "that's not a bad idea. It would give you a chance to get to know one of them better without the pressure of one-on-one time. You have to be at the wedding anyway, and Patrick and Jesse will probably take the day off. I doubt the Harts work many weekends."

When I think about it, they're right. Why not?

It might be nice to see how Patrick or Jesse behaves in that sort of setting. Weddings are the lifeblood of my business. Anyone I might date—or marry—will have to be comfortable attending them with me.

"Will you do it?" Ella asks.

I look over at Sonny, who gives me an enthusiastic thumbs up. We're probably giving that man ratings gold.

"Okay, okay," I say. "You twisted my arm. I'll do it. I'll invite one of them."

"Which one?" Clara asks.

I smile coyly, already knowing the answer. "Patrick," I say. "I want to get to know him better."

CHAPTER 12

PATRICK

Two Days Later

When Rosie invited me to attend the client's wedding with her, I was floored. That invite was probably the last thing I expected her to mention as we sat in her flower shop looking at floor plans and design schematics the other evening. Up until that point, the interaction had been strictly business.

I think Sonny knew it was coming, because he didn't act surprised. When he and I made eye contact, he wore a knowing grin.

Atta boy, Sonny.

I called Rosie the next evening, which was last night. We talked for more than an hour, mostly about the renovation and interior design in general, but towards the end of the conversation it began to feel like we were becoming friends. She might actually like me as a person. She might enjoy spending time with me.

I certainly feel the same way about her. She's every bit as wonderful as I'd thought.

Now, it's a beautiful, sunny Saturday morning and all the world seems bright. Flowers are in bloom, birds sing, and the smell of fresh-cut grass wafts through the air, delighting my senses. Truth be told, Loveland feels like home again.

I can't help but wonder if all of this was supposed to happen. It sort of seems like fate has me in its grips. I'm not complaining. Not if Rosalie Flowers is my destiny.

I'm dressed in one of my best suits and on my way to meet Rosie at The Romantics building. We'll load the flower arrangements into my car and head south to Chestnut Hill Lodge. Sonny and his crew will be there to film us loading, and they'll film at the wedding. But the time we spend in my car will be off camera. I can hardly wait.

On the drive over, I dial my dad. I wonder if he's heard about my love interest. Word spreads quickly around here. If he hasn't heard, I'll save the news for another time. He's still recovering from his illness, and I want to be sure he follows the doctor's orders to take it easy. He'd been out of the office for months. He's just now getting back into the swing of things.

"Good morning, son," he says when he answers.

"Hey, Dad," I reply. "How are you feeling?"

Dad's sister, my Aunt Gertrude, has been staying with him while he recovers. I hear her voice in the background. "Is that Patrick?" she asks. "Hi, Patrick!"

"Hi, Aunt Gertie," I say. "It's a beautiful spring day. Have you been outside?"

"Not yet," she replies, "but I was thinking about serving brunch on the patio."

"That sounds nice," I say. When my dad doesn't comment, I prompt him. "Doesn't it, Dad? Gertie is such a good cook."

His spirits have been down, which is understandable, given everything that's happened to him.

"Yeah," he says simply.

A silence stretches between us. I want to share my enthusiasm with him, but I don't even know what this thing with Rosie is yet. It doesn't seem like the right time to mention it. If he'd heard, I assume he would have said something right away. So, I move to a different subject.

"I'm going to a wedding today," I blurt, unsure how that will relate to anything useful.

"A wedding?" Dad asks. "What for?"

Good question. "I'm helping out, actually. With the flower arrangements. I'm sure it will be a nice time—at Chestnut Hill Lodge. The ceremony isn't until this evening, but I'm on my way to set up now."

"Do you know the couple?" he asks.

"Nope," I reply.

And now I know for sure that he hasn't heard anything about Rosie and me. If he had, the mention of flowers would have tipped him off.

"Well, have fun," he says. "But don't stay out too late. I need you at your best on Monday morning."

It makes me happy to hear the pride in his voice. He wanted me to join his firm for so long. Years. Maybe even decades, depending on how young I was when the thought first crossed his mind. I'm honored that he has that much faith in my abilities.

"I know, Dad," I say. "I won't let you down. I know how important the firm is to you. Jesse and I have taken good care of it while you were away. Now, we're eager to work alongside you during this new phase. This is our dream come true. We're building a Hart family legacy, together."

"I appreciate you boys," he says softly. "More than you know."

We say our goodbyes and I hang up the phone feeling relieved to hear Dad sounding strong. He's gaining more and more energy each day.

Rosie hasn't mentioned her mom to me yet, but knowing about her death and having faced the very real possibility of losing my dad puts things into a certain perspective.

Life is fleeting. It's important to make the most of the time we have.

I decide to focus on that effort today. I'm not sure what Rosie has in mind for this outing, but I intend to see that the day is a good one. Maybe even a day to remember many years from now, when I'm talking on the phone to our grown son.

There I go again, envisioning a future with Rosie. I can't seem to help it.

When I pull into the parking lot, my girl is waiting for me. She has a rolling cart loaded to the brim with boxed flower arrangements that she wheels over. Her hair is pulled into a sleek updo and she's wearing a brilliant orange dress that wraps around her every curve.

Pearl earrings and nude heels complete the look. She's absolutely stunning.

"Wow," I say when I greet her.

I lean over and kiss her cheek. It's a polite kiss, but when we touch it's charged with about a bazillion jolts.

Brandon warned me about this. He said I'd be ridiculously attracted to her, but that I should take things slow and spend time in conversation. I know he's right. I want to do this right. In fact, I told myself that I'd wait a week before even thinking about physical intimacy.

"What?" she asks playfully. "Haven't seen flowers this pretty before? Just wait until they're unboxed."

I fight the urge to scoop her into my arms. Instead, I chuckle, put my hands in my pants pockets, and rise onto my toes. "Haven't seen a *Ms. Flowers* this pretty before, that's for sure. You look positively gorgeous."

She smiles, and it lights up the already bright blue sky. "You don't look so bad yourself, Mr. Patrick Hart. The suit looks good on you."

I don't know what it is about her, but this woman is something else. I'm enamored with her. Transfixed. It's all I can do to turn away from her beauty when something else needs my attention. It isn't just her physical beauty, either. Her warmth and intelligence is inviting.

I load the boxes of flowers into my car as Rosie looks on, then she grabs several luggage bags and gets into the passenger seat. I don't know what's in the bags. Makeup and a change or two of clothes, if I had to guess. I don't care, really. If she wants them and they make her happy, I'll haul her bags anywhere.

"How has your morning been?" she asks thought-fully as we leave the parking lot and hit the winding road out of town.

"Good," I reply. "It's an awfully nice day. How was your morning?"

"Good," she replies.

We're still stiff. Still uncertain. It's okay. Rome wasn't built in a day. At least she isn't hating me, at the moment.

We chit chat while we drive, and it feels great to have time without cameras watching our every move. We talk about the weather, local news, and details of the wedding we're going to. We keep the conversation light. Nothing too personal. With every moment that passes, though, we're growing more comfortable with each other.

I'm learning her mannerisms—the way she bites her index finger when she's intrigued by something new, the way she grips the armrest when we go around a tight curve, and the way she seems most comfortable when she crosses her legs at the ankle, not the knee. These are the things a man should know about the woman in his life. I'm a dedicated and eager student.

"Would you look at that?" I ask as we pull past the black picket fencing and into the long driveway leading to what can only be described as a palatial estate.

I'd heard that Chestnut Hill Lodge was nice, but this is the first time I'm seeing it for myself.

"Have you been here before?" Rosie asks.

"Never. I guess a lot has changed in the time I've been away," I say.

She smiles, catching the deeper meaning. She doesn't hold eye contact for long, though. She has a job to do. I can tell she's getting her game face on.

"Follow this driveway to the lodge. It's the largest of the buildings up ahead, just past the dock on the pond," she says.

I do as I'm told, marveling at the grounds as we go. "What a beautiful place to get married," I muse.

"Yeah?" she asks as we park in the gravel lot near the lodge.

"Yeah."

We pause for a moment, admiring the view.

The lodge itself features a big A-frame roofline with wooden timbers flanking a mix of plank and stone. The natural colors they've chosen to place alongside each other are perfect against the green rolling hills in the background. Adirondack chairs sit huddled easy around a metal fire pit and add a welcoming touch. The whole place is sophisticated and elegant.

This is exactly the kind of place Hart Design+Build would create. I wonder if Dad had any part in this. He never mentioned it, so probably not. I make a mental note to use this as inspiration if our firm is ever hired to design something like it. From what I can tell, this place is markedly well done.

"Ready?" Rosie asks.

"When you are," I reply, cheerfully.

I take my cues from her. This is her scene, and I'm here to help. The last thing I want to do is get in the way. When she opens her car door and gets out, I follow along.

"What can I do?" I ask. "Is there a rolling cart here? Should I go get it?"

"Unfortunately, not one that can handle this gravel," she says. "We have to hoof it until we get into the building."

"No worries," I say. "I'm up to the task."

"Thank you, kindly," Rosie says, and her appreciation warms my heart.

We pick up as much as we can carry, then head inside with the first load. There are only a few cars in the parking lot, so I assume we have plenty of time.

"Looks like we beat the crowd," I muse as I balance the boxes and use one hand to open the door.

It's just as gorgeous inside the lodge as it is outside. Leather furniture, exposed brick walls, and huge wooden chandeliers make an impressive statement. We ooh and ahh over the interior for a moment, then get back to business.

"I like to be early," Rosie says. "That way, I'm always prepared. You know what they say about proper prior planning and all."

"I do," I reply. "I feel that way, too. Planning ahead keeps things simpler. I've found that I can avoid a lot of unnecessary difficulties that way."

"Same here," she says as we walk down a hallway toward the main hall where the ceremony is scheduled to take place this evening. "In here," she adds with a tilt of her head when we arrive at the right spot.

I turn and use my back to open the heavy wooden door. My arms are getting tired from carrying the boxes of flowers. I'm sure Rosie's are, too, even though her load is lighter than mine. "After you," I say, making space for her to walk past me.

When the door opens, I hear a weird hissing sound, followed by loud banging. It takes me a second to place it, but I do. Rosie's oblivious, though, too focused on her flowers to realize what's happening.

"Oh, no," I say with a laugh.

"What is it?"

The hissing turns into a moan, followed by a sucking sound. The banging continues. Literally.

Rosie blushes as the realization settles over her. "Maybe we're a little *too* early," she whispers. She closes her eyes, and I can't help but think how cute she looks with them that way.

"Maybe so," I agree. "Should we set these boxes down and make our exit?"

She nods, her eyes still closed.

From somewhere else in the room, a man's voice shouts, "Shut the door on your way out, would ya?"

"Sorry!" I call out.

We place the boxes on a table and scurry out the door. When we reach the hallway and close the big door behind us, we burst into laughter. We grasp each other's hands and Rosie leans her forehead against my chest as we laugh.

"Did we just hear what I think?" she asks.

"Yep. Pretty sure we did," I say. "Who was that?"

She can hardly talk now, she's laughing so hard. "I didn't get a good look—thank God!—but I believe it was the bride and groom, Stacy and Darius."

"I suppose it's their party—" I begin.

"And they can fuck if they want to," she adds, finishing my thought. "I'm just glad Sonny's camera crew isn't here yet. I swear, our TV show is going to be rated R for risqué. They might have to ship it to another network."

We howl with laughter as we jog back down the long hallway and out to my car. Now, I can tell for certain that this is going to be an event to remember.

CHAPTER 13

PATRICK

The ceremony goes off without a hitch.

Stacy and Darius manage to get themselves cleaned up and dressed up in time for their guests —and Sonny's camera crew—to arrive.

Every last detail of the wedding is perfect. The live music is moving, the flower girl and ring bearer are precious, and there isn't a dry eye in the house by the time the happy couple says their vows and their I Dos.

If you ask me, though, Rosie's flowers steal the show. The gardenias she worried so much over look amazing in the bouquets and as centerpieces on tables in the reception hall. I'm looking at them now, my belly full of wine from nearby Arrington Vineyards and locally smoked brisket.

"That was amazing," I say as I lean back in my chair.

I'm tempted to loosen my belt to allow for more breathing room, but I realize that would be a bad move. Rosie notices my change in posture.

"Feeling too full?" she asks.

I smile and reach for her hand, then stop myself. Sure, we touched earlier while laughing, but this is different. The mood is … different.

You can wait a week, Patch. Keep your attention on the conversation. Do as Brandon said.

"Something like that," I reply. "The food was good."

I can tell Rosie is more relaxed now. Her job is done. She can let herself be at ease.

"Are you ready to get out of here?" she asks, placing one hand on my knee and looking deeply into my eyes.

Whoa. Easy, girl.

"Not necessarily," I say.

I don't want to skip ahead. I definitely don't want Rosie to get physical with me because she thinks she should. I want her to know what kind of man I am. To know that this isn't some silly effort to replay my middle school glory days—if they could even be called that.

I want to do this properly.

She leans over to whisper in my ear, and my pants suddenly feel much tighter in the seat.

Oh, oh, oh.

Her scent is heavenly. Her skin looks soft and supple. Her voice … hell, don't get me started on her sultry, sexy voice.

"If we're staying a while longer, then dance with me, Patrick Hart," she says, her eyes daring.

I hesitate. What's the exit strategy here? If we dance, she'll be physically near me. I want that. Believe me, I *want* that. But I've committed to waiting a week. Not to mention, I'm not sure my suit coat is enough to hide the massive erection I'm likely to develop any minute now.

On the other hand, no way am I going to disappoint my girl when she wants to dance.

"Okay," I say, a lump in my throat. "Where's the dance floor?"

"Out back," she says, practically giddy. "Under the string lights on the patio. Tim McGraw is playing."

That gets my attention. "Tim McGraw? Seriously? *The* Tim McGraw?"

"Yeah, seriously. He lives around here, and he's a friend of the groom."

I nod, amazed.

"You know," she continues, "we have a lot of celebrities in the Nashville area. Especially in Loveland. Most of them are good folks, and us locals treat them with privacy and respect. We don't go all fangirling and making fools of ourselves."

"I get it," I say. "In fact, I like it. I love it …"

Rosie laughs, then continues the famous lyrics. "Let me guess … you want some more of it?"

"Exactly," she replies with a grin.

She stands, then takes my hand and leads me to the patio.

Sure enough, Tim McGraw's smooth voice greets us as we join the crowd dancing to the acoustic rendition of his mega hit, "I Like It, I Love It." Tim smiles and tips his hat to us as we walk past the stage and find a cozy spot to occupy on the dance floor.

"Tim McGraw," I muse as I place my hands on Rosie's hips. "I'll be damned. He's one of my all time favorites. His wife, Faith, too. They're country music royalty. I knew they lived around here, but I never thought I'd be in the same room with either of them."

She softens in my hands.

Oh, boy.

"Now you *can* meet him," she says. "After."

I'm not sure I'll make it to "after" without blowing a gasket. Rosie is driving me crazy. I'm doing my best to pretend she's not, but she'll know the truth soon. Once another inch or so of space closes between us, she'll feel it. She'll feel *me*.

"Yeah?" I ask, at a loss for more intelligent words.

She nods, then scoots close and nuzzles into my neck. "Yeah, Patrick Hart."

She does feel me, just as the song changes and Tim begins to sing "I Need You." I open my mouth to say something—to apologize—but she raises a finger to my lips to stop me.

"Hold me," she says.

I do, my body pressed firmly against hers as Tim sings about making love and needing his woman.

I'm about to lose my ever-loving mind.

As if things weren't already insanely magical, Rosie wraps one long, luscious leg around my waist and does some kind of backward dip. Apparently, she knows how to dance. And I mean, *really* dance. Is there anything she can't do?

I close my eyes, thanking the heavens above for the opportunity to be with her like this right now.

Just when I think I can't get more enchanted—or more aroused, let's call it like it is—a disturbance develops at the back edge of the patio, near a tree line. Angry shouting rises above the sound of Tim's music. There must be over a hundred people out here. They all turn toward the scuffle.

Tim stops playing his guitar, then waves for his band to do the same. "What's happening back there?" he asks, over the mic. We strain our necks to get a look.

In the moment that follows, we hear a voice that can immediately be recognized as belonging to someone who is intellectually or developmentally disabled. The man is screaming at the top of his lungs.

"You made him spray me! That wasn't nice! You are mean. All of you. You are mean, mean people," he says.

Another moment later, the distinctive foul scent of skunk wafts through the crowd and burns our noses. It's strong, like it was sprayed very close by. Several people scream. Many run indoors, waving their hands in front of their noses as they flee the stench.

"You're the retard who believed us!" a second voice can be heard saying. "Only retards think you can pet a skunk."

A third, unfortunate voice follows. "Now you smell like a skunk! *Retard*!"

More male voices laugh. I can't see the figures clearly in the dim light from this far away, but it looks like they're pointing cruelly, enjoying the suffering they've caused. They're making fun.

The disabled man bursts into tears, the sound of his heavy sobs drowning out everything else. He drops to the ground and curls into a fetal position.

Rosie and I part, and she looks at me as if she's searching for something.

I don't take time to think it over. I spring into action. "Stay here," I say.

My hands ball into fists as I march toward the oppressors. I soon pick up the pace into a run as the adrenaline pumps through my veins.

When I reach the asshole who is leading the charge, I punch him so hard in the face that he crumples to the ground, unconscious. Blood spews from his nose. I shake my fist, prepping for round two as I look for the second offender.

Before I can raise a hand to strike, Tim McGraw appears. He's there, at my side. He quickly locates the second man and grabs him, pinning the guy's arms behind his back. I instantly realize what Tim is doing. He's holding the man so that I can deliver a punch without fear of getting hit in the process. I clock the second guy just as hard as I did the first one.

Tim and I nod at each other and narrow our eyes, ready for more.

The rest of the cronies scatter, but we chase them down, giving each one the same treatment—Tim holds them steady while I give them a strong punch in the face.

Onlookers groan as they watch. Some cheer. Others seem to be disgusted by the show of violence.

"Why don't you let karma take care of these guys?" a lady from the crowd asks.

Tim winks at me, satisfied, and says, "We are karma, ma'am. My friend and I intend to make sure these boys don't pick on anyone who can't fight back ever again."

Huh.

"Damn straight," I reply.

I wipe the blood from my knuckles on the sides of my pants, then reach out for Tim's hand to shake it.

"Do you think they received the message?" Tim asks with a laugh.

"I'd say so."

"I guess they weren't around earlier when I sang 'Humble and Kind,' were they?" he asks, amused yet serious at the same time.

I shake my head and chuckle. "Doubt it, but they should listen on repeat."

We don't stick around to chat, though. Not yet. A quick glance between us communicates what's next.

Tim and I rush to the disabled man's side and crouch down to comfort him. The smell of skunk is terribly strong. It seems like the man took a direct hit at close range. He's rubbing his eyes, as if they burn. The poor guy.

I pull a clean, white handkerchief out of my pocket and hand it to the man as Tim puts a hand on his shoulder.

"We've got you, buddy," Tim says gently.

"That's right," I add. "Those boys are gone. They won't bother you again. You're safe."

The man's sobs slow as he listens. "They went away?" he asks.

"They did," I reply.

"I'm Bobby," the man says. "I'm scared."

I wrap my arms around Bobby's shoulders, doing my best to comfort him. "You're okay. It's okay."

A large crowd has gathered around us by now and is watching helplessly.

"Can someone get us some water?" I ask.

A female voice rises, "A bottle? Or can it be in a glass?"

"Any water will do," I say.

She hands me a glass full, and I get to work wetting the handkerchief.

Tim jumps in with further instructions. "Someone go to the kitchen and tell them we need tomato juice! As much of it as you can get your hands on."

"On it," a man says, then darts off.

By this point, Tim and I are covered in skunk ourselves. It's foul, but neither of us care. It feels good to do the right thing. We took care of business, and we'll stay with Bobby until we can get him cleaned up and home safe.

When Rosie's face appears in the crowd, it's covered in tears.

"Are you all right?" I ask, concerned. I don't take my arm away from Bobby.

I hadn't noticed Sonny's crew out here, but now I see them. They're bunching up behind Rosie, cameras hoisted on their shoulders.

"I'm right as rain," she says.

"What then?"

She shakes her head then wipes her eyes, allowing a big smile to form. "Patrick Hart," she says, "You've grown up to be a good man. I'm so very proud of you."

CHAPTER 14

ROSALIE

Friday
Six Days Later

I'm sitting at a desk in my flower shop when my mobile phone rings. It's an unknown number. I don't typically answer those, but something tells me I should pick this one up. It might be an important call.

I raise a finger in the air towards Rachael as I turn my back for privacy and answer the phone. She already knows I'm taking the afternoon off. Hopefully, she'll tend to her own business. I love her, but don't want to get into a big, serious conversation right now. I have a lot on my mind.

"Hello, Rosalie Flowers here," I say as I place the device against my ear.

I raise a shoulder and an ankle in a flirty pose when I hear the voice on the other end of the line. It's Patrick.

He's calling from the desk phone at his office, hence the unknown number. He wants to meet me right away.

It's been six days since I saw him at the Chestnut Hill Lodge wedding. For some reason, he insisted that we not see each other until this weekend. We've talked on the phone every day, but only about the renovation. It doesn't make any logical sense to me. He promised it wasn't anything bad, though. He said he wanted to give our relationship a little breathing room before becoming more personal. I figured I might as well believe him. At least, he's thinking things through.

"Now?" I ask, the alphabet soup effect from the first day we reunited returning to my mouth. "I thought we weren't getting together until tomorrow."

Patrick insists. He wants to see me a day early. I tell him I have some shopping to do, and he offers to come along. I don't argue, because my body wants to be near him. It feels warm and gooey again.

We agree to meet at Humboldt's Sandwich Shop downtown. We'll get a bite to eat, then Patrick will tag along while I shop for an outfit to wear on my date ... with his brother Jesse.

Don't judge me.

The date with Jesse doesn't have to mean anything, unless I want it to. I'm simply fulfilling an obligation. Keeping my word.

What could go wrong?

CHAPTER 15

ROSALIE

The sun is shining when I arrive at Humboldt's, big pretty rays that make the town look like it belongs in a Hallmark movie. Days like these are some of my favorites. Bright sun always feels hopeful, as if anything is possible.

I'm glad I've built my business to the point that I can take an afternoon off to enjoy myself every now and then. The Romantics building is just a few blocks from downtown, so I walked. It probably would have taken just as long to start up my car and drive over, anyway.

Sweet smells from the sandwich shop greet me with a burst as I open the heavy glass door and step inside. A bell rattles overhead to announce my entrance.

The lunch hour is drawing to a close, so the place is mostly empty. Waiters and waitresses are busy wiping down tables under shiny, red pendant lamps and bustling around behind the counter to clean up after the rush.

I tap my shoes on the entry mat to knock off some

dirt, then I take my crossbody handbag off, careful not to mess up my hair. I'm tousling my wavy locks to give them some volume when I see him.

Patrick is sitting at a table in the back, and he has his suit coat draped over the chair beside him. It's similar to the suit he was wearing last weekend at the wedding, only this one doesn't smell like skunk. The new view of his arms and shoulders gives me butterflies. He's physically fit all right. Fit as a fiddle. He must work out. But it's more than that. Clearly, good genetics are on his side.

It may sound silly, but I'm overwhelmed with the urge to hug him. And I mean a cuddly hug, where his big, strong arms are wrapped tightly over top of me and I can burrow down as I lean my head on his chest underneath.

I can't explain the urge. It still feels like I should be hating him.

"Rosalie!" Patrick calls when he notices me. "Back here. I ordered us some finger foods. Are you hungry?"

"Starving," I manage as I head to the back of the shop, hoping I don't trip along the way.

I feel like a baby deer on new legs again. Patrick has a strange effect on me.

"I wasn't sure what you'd like, so I ordered a few different things: vegetables with hummus, potato chips with a melted cheese dip, and salad. You can choose your dressing. Lindy there, the friendly young lady behind the counter, will get you whatever you want. I come here a lot. She knows me."

I look over at Lindy, who must be in her seventies.

She beams hearing Patrick describe her as a young lady.

So, he's good with the grandmotherly set, too. Noted.

"That's sweet. Ranch dressing would be great on the salad if they have it," I say as I remove my sunglasses from their perch on top of my head. I'm wearing a light sweater, and I move to take it off as well.

"Coming right up!" Lindy confirms. "We have a house made buttermilk ranch that's to die for."

She seems happy to oblige.

Patrick stands up to help with my sweater, like a gentleman. He walks around behind me and carefully slides my hair out of the way before tugging my sweater down the length of my arms.

I'm not usually big on chivalry. In fact, I've been known to tell men that I don't need their help when they try to open doors for me. I used to complain to Jimmy about it all the time. I didn't want to be seen as helpless. I'm not some damsel in distress who needs saving.

But for some reason, I like a bit of chivalry coming from Patrick. It doesn't feel condescending. To the contrary. It makes me feel cared for.

"There," he says softly as he places my sweater on top of his on the chair, and I stand awestruck. He is really nice.

I don't think I got this close to him in my flower shop, but I'm reminded of being near him last weekend at the wedding. He smells amazing. If I had to describe his scent, I'd say it's an alluring mixture of pine sap and leather … if there is such a thing.

Whatever it is, my body is responding. This man is oh, so sexy.

"Have a seat," Patrick prompts, motioning towards the chair across from him.

I glance at the seat beside him instead. The one with the coat and sweater.

"Unless you want to sit over here next to me," he says with a jovial smile. "That's mighty forward of you, Ms. Flowers. But I'm on board."

I feel my cheeks turning colors.

I have a lousy poker face. People can usually tell exactly what I'm thinking. My friends say it's an endearing quality. At this particular moment, I'm not so sure.

"Come on," Patrick encourages. "I saw you looking at the chair."

"Oh, yeah," I mutter. "I was just looking at our garments, there. I wouldn't want them to slide off onto the floor."

I silently scold myself. What kind of excuse was that? *Rosalie! Get. It. Together.*

Patrick smiles and leans back in his chair, apparently amused.

"Do I make you nervous?" he asks, definitely amused.

He tilts his head to one side and I find myself looking at his plump, luscious lips again. Even a quick glance at those lips causes me to lose complete track of what I'm supposed to be doing. Time stands still. It sounds cliche, but I'm serious. Something is happening. I don't think a man has ever made me this discombobulated.

Dammit, Patrick.

"Are you nervous, Rosalie?"

"Oh, no," I sputter, taking a deep breath as I work to regain my composure … that is, if I ever had my composure to begin with. "I'm fine."

"You certainly are *fine*," he says, dragging the last word out and taking a slow glance up and down my figure. "And you want to sit by me. It must be my lucky day."

"Oh …"

I can't seem to find any words that will leave my mouth properly. My speaking vocabulary has regressed to that of a toddler.

Patrick stands and moves the coat and sweater to the seat across from him, then he wraps one arm around my waist and guides me to the chair beside his. I let him do it. I'm not sure I have it in me to resist. My skin warms another ten degrees at his touch. My blood is pumping. I wonder if his is too.

He's different than he was at the wedding. I mean, he's the same, but he seemed to be holding back then. Not anymore.

"That's better," he whispers in my ear as we sit.

He pulls my chair close to his and lets his arm rest along the back. His warm body beside mine feels oddly like home.

"Hummus?" he asks as he uses his free hand to dip a carrot stick in the mushy stuff.

"Sure," I say.

Patrick raises the carrot to my mouth. I wasn't expecting that move, but it's surprisingly intimate. *Huh.* Who would've thought hummus could be sexy?

I take a bite, Patrick's fingers slowly brushing against my lips. Then I suddenly burst out laughing, nearly choking on my carrot stick.

"What?" he says, wanting in on the joke.

"It's just a movie I'm thinking of … the hummus …" I try, still laughing.

Patrick chuckles. "Is it *You Don't Mess with the Zohan,* by chance? Because it cracks me up every time I think about Adam Sandler brushing his teeth with hummus."

"Yes! How did you know?" I ask. "It's hilarious."

"I agree!"

Thank God, the tension has been broken. Thanks to hummus, of all things. Well … there's still sexual tension between us. But it's a more welcome tension, at least. The awkwardness is beginning to subside.

"Are you a movie buff?" I ask.

"I guess I am," Patrick replies. "I seem to find myself at the movie theater at least once a week. How about you?"

He moves his hand off the chair and onto my shoulders as he talks. I melt into him and lean closer.

"Same," I say. "Although it's more like once every couple of weeks for me. I do a lot of streaming movies at home. My cat …"

I stop myself, not wanting to sound like a crazy cat lady.

"Go on," he prompts. "What's your cat's name?"

"Tabatha," I reply. "A tabby."

"Nice."

Jimmy used to complain about Tabatha. He hated cats. But Patrick, on the other hand, doesn't seem phased. Noted. I'd love nothing more than to curl up on my couch with Patrick and Tabatha each night after a long day of work. Sounds heavenly.

"I used to have a cat," Patrick explains. "Goose was his name. For a long time, it was me, Goose, and my dog, Maverick."

"Aw, what happened to Goose?" I ask, leaning so close that my lips could touch his with the slightest movement.

He doesn't pull away.

"Old age," he explains.

I can feel his warm breath on my face now.

"It was the big guy's time," he continues. "The natural course of things. I sure do miss him though. He was a tabby, too. Grey. A gorgeous animal."

"Tabatha is gray, with a white chest and feet. It looks like she's wearing tiny mittens."

"Sounds darling," Patrick replies.

We look at each other, and I could swim in his rich brown eyes. I think he might kiss me. I arch my back in anticipation. But I lose my nerve and turn my head.

"And Maverick?" I ask. "What kind of dog is he?"

"A coonhound. Big and goofy. He's loyal, though. And protective."

I nod, then pick up a celery stick and scoop it in the hummus.

"I've always wanted a big dog," I say as I chew. "To protect me."

"Yeah?"

"Yeah."

"Do you need protection?" he whispers, leaning close to my ear. "Because that … I could provide."

It sends shivers up and down my spine and I think I might jump his bones right here and now.

There's a bathroom in this place. We could sneak in quietly and devour each other. Lindy would probably smirk. But she wouldn't tell. And even if she did, I'm not sure I'd care. The cameras aren't here. I want Patrick's big hands on my skin in the most delicate places. I want his lips on my neck. I want to feel him pressed tightly up against me, without these pesky clothes in between us.

I've never romped with a man in a bathroom before. Do I sound crazy?

It's not like Patrick and I are strangers. We've known each other for as long as I can remember. My parents knew his parents. Our moms volunteered on the PTA together. Our dads played racquetball against each other at the athletic club. That kind of history has to count for something.

Lindy brings my salad dressing to the table, and Patrick puts some distance in between us. I don't want him to move an inch, but we are in a sandwich shop in the middle of the day, after all. We should probably tone it down before someone tells us to get a room.

We thank Lindy in our best normal-sounding voices, even though we're both hot and bothered.

Patrick takes his arm back and we eat in silence.

Everything tastes wonderful. Probably due to the—ahem!— mood we're in. My whole world looks shiny right now. The endorphins are flowing. And they're not the only thing flowing. My panties are soaked with slippery goodness. I feel delectably wet and ready.

"Should I order us sandwiches?" Patrick asks, his voice proper.

A family with three young kids has just come in. We will definitely have to tone it down now, or move to a second location.

"Sure," I say. "I have an appetite for meat." I let the words hang in the air. "You know, for the protein."

I can hardly believe I actually said that. I'm sort of proud of myself. My flirting game is strong. Or *stronger*, anyway. Maybe? I deserve some kind of award for Most Improved, at least.

Go, Rosalie.

But in all seriousness, I do need some protein to eat. I need to keep my head on straight, and I won't feel as good without something more solid than vegetables and hummus in my stomach.

"Listen to you," Patrick says with a smile and a wink.

"We could share something," I suggest.

"Sure. What suits you?" he asks.

"My answer might change later," I say, resting one hand on his knee and giving it a squeeze. "But for now, a turkey sandwich will hit the spot. Want to split one?"

Patrick agrees. We eat our food quickly, eager to get out of Hemboldt's and see what the rest of the afternoon holds.

I nearly forget about Jesse altogether. But a promise is a promise, and I'm committed to keeping my date with him tonight. Like I told Clara and Ella, Jesse asked me first.

"Are you sure you want to tag along while I shop?" I ask Patrick before we get up from the table. "It will be boring. That is, unless waiting for a woman to try on clothes is your idea of a good time."

He wrinkles his nose like the idea tickles him. "Might I get a glimpse of said clothes as you try them on?" He smiles a devilish smile, and I go all warm and gooey again.

"You might," I say coyly. "I suppose that isn't too much to ask."

"Good!" Patrick exclaims. "Then it's a date."

CHAPTER 16

ROSALIE

The sunshine keeps coming as we walk arm-in-arm along a sidewalk downtown. And nearly every thought that crosses my mind sounds sexual.

I'd like to keep coming. I suspect Patrick could make that happen for me.

I don't ask him where his car is parked or what he might be missing at work this afternoon. I don't mention our adversarial relationship when we were kids either. I don't want anything to interrupt our time together in the here and now. It's downright wonderful, if I do say so myself.

I'll admit I feel guilty not telling Patrick I have another date. Especially since the date is with his brother. But I push that out of my mind, content to live in the moment. I'm all aglow since Patrick called what we're doing a date. It feels more official now.

I catch a glimpse of our reflection as we pass by a glass-front furniture shop. I really like the way we look together. We're an attractive couple. And we look as happy as can be.

Dare I say it ... but it looks like we *go* together. Like we *belong* together.

Oh, be still, my heart.

I'm a romantic. And not just by nickname.

I almost named my flower shop Bloom by Bloom because I love the idea of using flowers to celebrate life's big moments, one bloom at a time. I ended up going with Rosalie's Flowers because it was too easy, given my name. But I still have my sights set on using Bloom by Bloom somehow. Maybe it could be a delivery service for important days ... like for the sweet stories you hear about people setting up flower delivery for their loved ones years after they've passed away. It seems a name like Bloom by Bloom would be a daily reminder of why I do what I do. I make a mental note to work it in somehow.

I could have chosen any occupation, but flowers are the most meaningful things I could think of. The fact that my last name is Flowers is just a bonus. Serendipity, maybe.

"Ooohh," Patrick says as he stops suddenly and pulls me into a store.

As luck would have it, it's Taylor's, the only other flower shop in Loveland. We're competitors, but we're friendly with each other. They tend to let me have more of the wedding industry business. They take care of most of the funerals. And school dances. Anything other than weddings, really.

"What are we doing?" I ask as we stop in the

entryway and Patrick guides me to a spot beside a bench.

"Sit down, and stay here," he says excitedly. "I'll be right back."

A look of confusion stays on my face, but I do as I'm told. I wonder what he's up to.

"Oh," he calls back. "Close your eyes!"

"You can't be serious," I say.

"I am! Keep them closed. I'll be back before you know it."

Whatever, silly.

I nod my head as my eyes slide shut. I have no idea what Patrick is doing. But I feel like a kid at Christmas as I wait to find out ... Until doubts begin to race through my mind. I try my best to push them away.

What if Patrick deserts me right here in my competitor's shop? I'll be the talk of the town. What if this is too heavy or too fast for him, and he wants to bail? I wouldn't blame him. Jimmy felt that way, apparently. At least, Patrick would be getting it over with quickly rather than drawing it out ... and cheating on me.

It's unsettling how vulnerable I feel sitting here with my eyes closed. Maybe I'm in over my head. Maybe I like this guy so much, it scares me.

Dammit, Rosalie. Get. Yourself. Together.

I'm still talking myself down when I feel a warm hand on mine.

It's Patrick. I recognize his touch already. And those hands ... I want them to be mine.

"Rosie, sweet," he whispers as he scoops me up into his arms. "Open your eyes."

I open my eyes, and my heart melts when I see.

He's holding a corsage in one hand … the kind you wear on your wrist to a middle school dance. It has five white roses, three pink peonies, and blue privet berries with green foliage as accent. It's beautiful. Exactly what I'd pick out for myself.

Swoon.

"Roses for my Rosie," Patrick says as he slips the corsage on.

I look over his shoulder, and Mike Taylor, the shop manager, is standing behind us with a portable speaker. He's wearing a proud grin on his face. A trio of customers looks on. They're smiling too.

"May I have this dance?" Patrick asks me as he begins to sway. "I promise this one won't end with skunk and a fist fight. This is about going way back."

He wraps one arm around me and pulls me tightly against him as he holds my other hand with the corsage between us and against his chest.

Mike pushes the button to start the music as I mumble my yes.

Ellie Goulding's voice fills the room as she sings "How Long Will I Love You" above a romantic piano melody. Her lyrics say she'll love him as long as stars are above, and she'll need him as long as seasons need to follow their plan. Every single word envelopes me, and I fall deeper and deeper.

Patrick is romancing me. And he's doing a bangup job.

"What is all this?" I ask quietly as we dance.

"Do you remember our eighth grade formal?" he asks.

"Of course," I reply.

Patrick had asked me to be his date. Stupidly, I thought he was serious, but it turned out to be a prank. He stood me up. Then a group of his juvenile-delinquent friends laughed in my face. I was mortified.

"I owe you an apology," he continues. "A big one."

He leans his cheek against mine and nuzzles my face as he explains.

"That was a million years ago," I say. "No need …"

"Stop," he says sweetly. "What I did was terrible. I'm so sorry. I hope you can forgive me."

"I think …"

He raises our clasped hands and puts a finger up to my lips. "Just listen," he says, nuzzling against me again.

"Okay."

"It isn't just the dance that I need to apologize for. I was a real brat. I gave you a hard time, and I know it."

I nod, gently.

"The truth is … I was enamored with you. You were my childhood crush. The object of my desire. The girl of my dreams. I teased you because I didn't know how to handle my feelings. And I asked you to that dance because I really liked you. But then I was too much of a wus to go through with it. I'm sorry, Rosie. If you'll let me, I'd like to spend my days making it up to you."

I try to move my head to look at him, but he pulls me back.

"Shh," he says. "There's more."

Our bodies move in sync as Ellie Goulding continues her serenade via Mike's speaker. Tears drip from my eyes. I'm overwhelmed.

"When we moved to Georgia, I promised myself that I'd come back to Loveland and find you one day," Patrick explains. "I didn't want to be creepy about it. It's not like I stalked you or anything."

We both chuckle.

"Patrick …" I breathe. "I liked you too. I *like* you …"

"Then it sounds like fate brought us back together," he says in the sexiest voice I've ever heard in my entire life. "I've waited for today. I knew it would come. And now, here we are."

"Here we are," I echo as I move my mouth to his.

I part my lips ever so slightly, tilting my head and closing my eyes. He moves slowly, savoring the moment.

Could this be our last first kiss?

When Patrick finally places his exquisite lips on mine, I feel like I might just float up and away. This is bliss.

Mike and his customers clap and cheer as Patrick and I become intertwined, our tongues exploring each other in a sensual dance of their own.

I can feel Patrick's manhood protruding from his trousers and reaching out for me, just like it did at the wedding last weekend. It was all I could do to resist him then. I won't be able to do it again.

He wants me. And I want to be wanted—body, mind, and soul.

As beautiful as this moment is, I'm anxious to get to some place more private.

"Patrick, baby," I say softly, pressing my hips into his and nuzzling his nose. "Let's get out of here."

He smiles and pulls me even closer. "Your wish is my command, Rosie. I'd follow you anywhere."

My name sounds so good when he says it.

We bid farewell to Mike and his customers, then we enjoy one more warm kiss before bounding out into the sunshine, hand in hand.

CHAPTER 17

ROSALIE

"Where to?" Patrick asks with a grin. "I don't want to distract from your shopping."

"Forget about shopping," I say, turning around and walking backwards so I can see his handsome face in front of mine. "My place is about a block from here. I'll just pick something from my closet to wear tonight. I can try things on, and you can give me your opinion."

I'm still committed to the date with Jesse simply to honor my obligation, but I've become far less concerned about what I wear.

"Oh, really?" Patrick says, kissing me between words. "You live downtown?"

Haven't we discussed this? I'm pretty sure he already knows, but I'll play along.

"I do."

"That's funny, because I do, too," he says. "My place is about a block from here, but in the other direction.

Fourth Avenue. Truth be told, though, I'd rather live in a farmhouse out on some land. Condo living is hard on a big ol' coonhound like Maverick."

My earlier visions of remodeling a farmhouse while I pat my pregnant belly come flooding back. Only this time, Maverick is galloping along behind Patrick, wagging his tail. A tiny, spotted puppy prances along as well. I swear to everything that's holy, I've never thought about such a future before.

At least, not the pregnant belly part. Or the coonhound part. Maybe just the spotted puppy.

"Did someone tell you all the right stuff to say today?" I tease. "Let me guess. Was it Clara? That little do-gooder can't help herself. She probably told you all the things I like."

Patrick laughs as I right myself and walk forward.

"Nope," he says, getting a kick out of my inquisition. "I haven't seen Clara Darling or Ella Lovelace since the summer before ninth grade."

"Are you sure about that?" I ask.

"What? Can't things flow between us without a hidden reason why? When we were kids, I studied you like a textbook. I know more about you than you probably realize."

"Flow is nice," I confirm. "It's just a lot to take in."

Patrick stops and looks at me in mock protest, beads of perspiration lining his forehead from the heat.

"But in a good way," I add enthusiastically. "Come on. I'll show you to my humble abode. I'm on Second Avenue."

We walk together towards my building, chatting happily about what we've each been up to all these years. Rays of golden sunshine continue to blanket the town around us.

I wrap my sweater gently over my wrist to protect the corsage from the wind. I don't want it to get destroyed. When it begins to wilt, I intend to hang this little beauty upside down so that it can dry out. Then I'll press it in one of my favorite old books and keep it forever. It's the best gift anyone has ever given me. Maybe I'll show it to our kids one day.

Did I really just think that?

As we talk, I find out Patrick's dad is remarried to a woman from Pennsylvania. His mom still lives in Atlanta with her second husband. The four parental figures get along well and even spend holidays together sometimes. It sounds like the elder Harts made it through that divorce relatively unscathed. Patrick tells me he's happy for them, but doesn't want his life to turn out the same way. He intends to get married once to the right woman, then grow old and gray with her.

I swoon again hearing him talk about it. He sounds so certain. So sincere.

I tell Patrick about attending college in Virginia and graduating with a degree in business, then coming back to Loveland and opening my flower shop. I tell him about Clara, Ella, and I going into business together and how we've remained close, like sisters.

He explains that he went to Athens, Georgia for college at UGA, completing his degree in architecture and then working at a firm in Atlanta before returning to Loveland a few months ago to join up with his dad. He says he never stopped thinking about me, even going so far as to look me up online from time to time.

I tell him that I've loved and lost, but that no relationship has ever felt quite right. He says the same, and he sounds convinced there is a good reason why. I'm beginning to think so, too.

Maybe we belong together.

When we arrive at my building and climb the stairs behind the bakery to the second floor, we practically run down the hallway, eager to get inside and away from prying eyes. Patrick pinches my butt playfully as I fumble with the keys in the lock.

The chemistry between us is incredibly hot. Like, off the charts hot. Hotter than anything I've experienced before.

I have a feeling that once Patrick and I really get our hands on each other, it will eclipse every single memory of Jimmy and the shoulder rubs set against the twin-kling lights of Nashville.

Once we're in my condo and the door slams shut behind us, Patrick and I tear at each other's clothes hungrily. I'm sure we look like a couple from a sex scene in an x-rated movie. I don't mind. I'm sure it's a good look for us.

It certainly feels good. I don't think I've ever felt more alive.

Bewildered by the intrusion, Tabatha steps in between us and meows loudly.

"Excuse you," I say sternly to my cat.

Patrick and I chuckle as he bends down to scratch her under the chin.

"So, this is the Tabatha I've heard about. She's a good girl. Isn't she?"

Tabatha purrs, enjoying the attention. She instantly likes Patrick. She's an excellent judge of character.

"She is a good girl, but a pushy one," I say to Patrick, twirling a lock of his short hair between my fingers.

Having his head at the same level as my— well, *lady bits*— drives me wild. I want his sensual mouth on both my pairs of lips, and the lower ones positively ache for him. They want a taste.

He turns his head my way, stopping just inches short of those very same lady bits as he talks to Tabatha.

"You're a sweetie," Patrick says to her. "But you're not the only pussy I intend to meet today."

He stands up, and in one fluid motion lifts me onto the nearby dining table as my long legs wrap greedily around him. He leans his eager member hard against me while he carefully shifts a spring-themed candle centerpiece over to one side of the table so that I can lean back without knocking it onto the floor.

I moan with anticipation as he moves. He's taking care of me in a way that's both aggressive and tender.

"Oh, Patrick …" I say, already breathless.

He kisses me deeply, raising my arms over my head, then he slides my sweater and pink tank off, careful not to disturb the corsage.

Gently, he unfastens my bra. Savoring the process, he leans down and takes one of my nipples into his mouth for a nibble and a lick before leaning back and smiling as he admires my exposed breasts.

"You are a beauty like no other, Rosalie Flowers."

My nipples are firm and taut, ready for his attention. They're aching almost as much as the rest of me. I'm aching for him.

I raise my hands, grabbing at my breasts and fingering the nipples as the corsage bounces against my skin. He watches intently, lust oozing from his pores while he saunters his thirsty shaft slowly and deliberately between my legs.

I'm ravenous for him.

It's as if my body is awakening to an ecstasy it's never known before. And I'm here for it. No place I'd rather be.

Patrick raises my skirt, burying his head beneath the deep pleats while I writhe with pleasure. He slides my leggings down carefully, then bites and tugs at my silk panties with his teeth, just forcefully enough to turn me on more and more with every touch.

I'm wetter than I knew possible, dripping with desire. Patrick laps my juices up as if I'm made of his favorite nectar, his lips and tongue slipping and sliding in my folds. I tousle his hair as I guide his head, my legs now bent with my feet on the table. The position gives me leverage for sensations that are way out of this world.

My body heaves from the stimulation, bursting with such force that it feels like I could blow the glass right out of the windows if I directed the energy that way.

"Oh my God!" I scream as I climax, my back arched

and my toes curled. "Patrick, baby! Oh, oh, oh …" I say as I kick the table in delight.

People in the bakery downstairs probably wonder what the hell is happening. Although, they shouldn't have to wonder. It's obvious. My clock has just been cleaned. My world has been rocked.

"That's my girl," Patrick says, taking a long, deep lick of me before standing up and pressing his wet lips against my mouth.

I've never orgasmed more than once in a love-making session, but I already know I'm going to today.

"Are you ready for more?" he asks seductively. "Because I have a whole lot of love for you."

He reaches down and unbuttons his trousers, then takes his rod out, gripping it hard.

It's big. And—*oh, my God*—thick, with the perfect mushroom head on top. I have a feeling that organ will fit like a glove, delving into every deep, throbbing part of me and activating pleasure centers I never knew I had.

"You're so wet and enticing," he says as he licks his lips. "I want to be inside you."

"Then come and get me," I reply, tilting my head back while I wait.

He lifts me again, my legs straddling him. This time he's more forceful. He's getting a feel for how rough I like it. And he's looking forward to his own release.

Patrick scans the condo for a bed, and I laugh.

"Hey now, give me a break," he says with a chuckle. "I've never been here before."

"Through the door, over there," I instruct, then I lean

down and nibble on one of his earlobes as he carries me. "I must say, you're making quite an impression for your first time."

"Maybe that's because I've imagined this day for so long," Patrick says.

"Aww."

"I'm serious. It's always been you, Rosie."

I smile as he places me gently down on the bed. It's made neatly, with plush pillows and a cozy quilt on top. Fresh peonies in three different shades of pink stand dutifully in a vase on my dresser.

"Well, would you look at that?" Patrick says when he sees the flowers. "Just like your corsage ... which looks amazing on you, by the way."

"Thank you, baby," I say. "And I know. That's why I asked if Clara and Ella had filled you in on what I like."

"I guess we're just in sync," he says, taking the rest of his clothes off and then slowly crawling on top of me.

His body is a work of art. Every inch of him is chiseled like a Greek statue. He's firm, but not too firm. I find him perfect, actually. His sexy soccer-player build is the physique I like most on a man. It feels like I've died and gone to heaven.

"I guess we are in sync," I agree. "I'm not complaining."

I'm still wearing my skirt. It's working for me. Being naked except for my skirt and corsage makes me feel fancy, like I'm dressed up for our first time making love. I want this to be special and memorable.

Patrick moves to unzip my skirt, but I stop him.

"Leave it," I say. "I like watching you work around it."

"Okay, then," he replies in a whisper. "I'd better get busy."

Sensing that I need a slower pace now, Patrick takes his time. He's a giver. He takes such exquisite care of me, gradually moving over every inch of my body as he plants warm kisses. I close my eyes and enjoy it.

With Jimmy, I kept score, always afraid I'd be accused of not doing my fair share. If he pleasured me for five minutes, I'd pleasure him for ten. This is different.

I feel completely at ease with Patrick. He takes as much pleasure in making me feel good as he does receiving. Maybe more.

I didn't know this was even possible.

Patrick, where have you been all my life? Oh, yeah. You were a snot-nosed kid torturing me for a decent part of it.

I laugh out loud.

"What's so funny?" he asks, rounding one of my hips on his way back to the front.

"Nothing, really," I say.

"Come on, sweet," he says seductively. "I want to laugh with you."

This man is really something.

"I was laughing at my own thoughts," I explain. "I wondered where you've been all my life, then immediately remembered that you were there for a lot of it … You know, teasing the hell out of me."

"I know," he replies, leaning up on one elbow. "I'm glad you can laugh about it. I'm not sure I'm ready to laugh yet. I still feel terrible."

I pick up a pillow and toss it at him playfully.

"Hush," I say, pulling him in for a kiss. "Patrick Hart, shut up and make love to me."

"Yes, ma'am," he says with a wink.

Then he proceeds to deliver the most mind-blowing lovemaking session I've ever experienced.

I'll never be the same.

CHAPTER 18

ROSALIE

I'm sprawled out on the bed, completely spent, when my phone dings. Patrick is in the shower.

It's a text from Jay … err, Jesse. I haven't heard a peep from him in more than a week.

Shit. Shit. Shit.

What am I supposed to do about this little predicament? It's been months since mom died and Jimmy broke my heart. I haven't dated anyone. And now, I have two guys pursuing me. Brothers, no less.

This is insane.

It's comical, really. Jesse probably doesn't realize it's me. He probably doesn't know that he knows me. It was crowded and loud at the coffee stand when we met. The same way I thought I heard him say Jay, he might have heard me say Rosa, or I don't know … something other than his childhood acquaintance Rosalie Flowers. I'm not sure I mentioned my name.

I don't even know where he's taking me tonight. He

didn't say. The whole thing was super casual and low-key. I'm not sure what to wear.

Jesse's text asks where he should pick me up. I tell him to meet me at the Romantics building. Might as well keep things simple. Jesse doesn't necessarily need to know where I live. And he certainly doesn't need to run into Patrick here.

He replies his okay.

I place a hand on my head as I consider how to navigate the evening.

The last thing I want to do is hurt Patrick's feelings. I really, really like him. And I feel like this is the beginning of something real and true. But keeping my word to Jesse seems important. It's just a casual date. It doesn't need to mean anything more.

I have to text Clara and Ella. They're never going to believe how my afternoon went.

Then again, there isn't time. Patrick and I have been occupied with each other for hours now. I have about forty-five minutes to get cleaned up and over to the Romantics building to meet Jesse.

No big deal, Rosalie. Just go through the motions.

I hop out of bed, take off my skirt and corsage, and join Patrick in the bathroom.

"Hey, there, sweet," he says from the shower as he wipes shampoo bubbles off of his forehead. "Want to join me?"

I adore the way he calls me sweet.

"I'd love to," I say. "But I have a prior commitment tonight. I've got to get going soon."

"Boo, hiss," he jokes as he pulls me into the shower stall anyway. "It isn't soon yet."

"You devil you," I tease.

"Yeah, yeah," he says as he wraps his arms around me. "I have that thing at the firm tonight, anyway. Remember? I'll have to get going soon too. You sure you don't want to come with me? You're still invited."

"Truly, I can't. Or I would," I reply, leaning my head on Patrick's warm, wet chest.

He feels like home.

He sways gently, and we stay like that for what feels like forever, dancing in the shower. This really is heaven.

"When will I see you again?" Patrick asks quietly.

I sigh. Wishing I didn't have to leave him at all.

"I don't know," I say. "I'm not sure what time I'll be done tonight."

"Oh…"

"Oh, wait … I didn't mean … Maybe you were thinking about another day?" I ask, backpedaling.

I don't intend to sound presumptuous.

"No, I was thinking about tonight. I want to be with you, sweet. Whenever I can."

"Me, too," I say.

Patrick looks me in the eye. "Look," he assures. "We have the rest of our lives. I'm not going anywhere. There's no hurry. And no pressure."

I nod and smile. He's right. I should relax.

"So, you call me when you can," he confirms. "I have to tend to Maverick and show up to work from time to time, but otherwise, I'm available."

"I will," I promise.

Patrick gives me a squeeze, then steps out of the water and towels off. He gets dressed and leaves my condo while I shower, getting ready to do God knows what with Jesse.

I speed up the pace once Patrick is gone, blow drying my long hair and applying makeup. I'm a little disappointed that I ran out of time to try on clothes for Patrick, but I guess that's probably for the best. It would be weird if he'd helped me pick out an outfit for a date with his brother.

I select a blue maxi dress with a black belt bearing a gold buckle to cinch it in at the waist. I pair the dress with black high heels and a gold necklace.

I leave my hair down, brushed heavily to one side for a little drama. I glance outside, and it looks like the weather will stay nice. I can probably get through the evening without a sweater. It was too warm for one earlier, really.

I size myself up in the floor-length mirror on the back of my bedroom door. I look good. Maybe too good. I'm not sure I want attention from anyone but Patrick. At least, not until I'm officially his and can tell other men I'm taken.

I hurry out the door, filling Tabatha's food along the way and laughing again at Patrick's pussy comment.

Meow.

I lock the door behind me, then head out on foot. My car is still at the office. I don't mind, though. The fresh air helps me clear my head.

I've got to figure out how I'm going to play this. I

assume it isn't wise to tell Jesse that I know who he really is and—*Surprise!*—I just rolled out of bed with Patrick. Yeah, that's definitely not good.

So, what?

Maybe I'll pretend that I only know him as Jay from the coffee stand, and I'll keep quiet about the rest. I can get through the evening, then give "Jay" the let's-be-friends treatment. Once Patrick and I become an official couple and I see Jesse at a family function, I can play dumb.

Easy enough, right?

Except that I hate to lie. I rarely do it. I sometimes withhold strategic information, which is sort of lying … technically … but I don't just lie outright. It feels wrong. I'm not even sure if this little charade would count for my withholding-information cop out. It all depends on how tonight goes.

The parking lot at the Romantics building is nearly empty when I arrive. My little car sits where I left it, full of boxes and flower-related items, actually. I got distracted and forgot about the mess. It would take awhile to clear. Hopefully, Jesse has a vehicle ready.

I step inside the lobby, hoping for a few minutes with Clara and Ella—or Rachael—before Jesse arrives. I could use some friendly advice right now. And I have so much to tell them.

But no such luck.

Jesse is there waiting for me. He's wearing a black and white tweed coat over a button down shirt and black pants.

He looks good. Damn good. Better than I remember.

Shit. Shit. Shit.

This would have been easier if he'd shown up looking frumpy. Or out of shape. Or … anything other than … this.

"There you are," he says warmly. "You look nice."

"Hey! Thanks." I reply awkwardly, raising my hand in a motion like I'm tipping an invisible hat.

Here we go again.

I'm such a dork.

Jesse laughs. His laugh sounds a lot like Patrick's.

"Are you ready?"

It's a simple question on the surface, but one I scarcely know how to answer.

I hesitate, finally saying, "Sure. Let's do this."

"All right, then," he confirms, gesturing towards the exit. "Want to ride with me?"

I walk through the door he's holding open, silently scolding myself for accepting all of this chivalry. It doesn't feel quite as good coming from Jesse. I think … I feel sort of loyal to Patrick's chivalry.

Noted.

"That works," I confirm. "My car is full of flower stuff, so I might as well. Where are we going?"

"I thought we'd start with dinner," he explains. "Are you hungry?"

"Yes, I am," I reply.

I'm famished, actually. This afternoon's—ahem!—physical exertion worked up quite an appetite.

"There's a sushi place down on Elm Street I frequent. How does that sound?"

I hate sushi. Not sure I could choke it down if I had to.

"Oh … Hmm …"

"What? You're not a fan?" Jesse asks as he opens the passenger door of his car for me.

"Yeah, I'm not big on sushi," I say. "Sorry."

He wrinkles his lip slightly as he closes the door behind me and walks around to the other side.

"Thai?" he asks as he gets himself situated in the driver's seat.

"I could do that," I reply.

"Huh …" he says. "You don't sound enthused."

"I'm sorry," I say again.

Why am I apologizing?

"Asian food in general isn't my favorite. But I can eat it."

"Okay, good enough. Thai it is."

Good enough? Really? Patrick wouldn't say good enough. He'd take me wherever I wanted to go.

Jesse puts the car in gear and we're off.

I'm afraid this will be a long, difficult night.

CHAPTER 19

PATRICK

I practically bounce out of the car as I arrive home at my condo to change for the office party happening tonight. Brandon is waiting for me. He's in town for another few days before heading back to Atlanta. I'm eager to tell him about my afternoon.

I open the front door, and Maverick saunters over to greet me.

"Hey, big guy!" I say, more cheerfully than usual. "Who's a good boy? Maverick is a good boy, isn't he? *Isn't* he?"

My dog can tell I'm amped up. He does a quick turn and dance, matching my energy. I scratch him behind the ears. He smiles as best a dog can, then leans into me —his version of an embrace.

"Brandon?" I call as I drop my keys into a bowl on the entryway table and make my way to the living room.

The room has a scenic view of the rolling hills and

river in the distance. Brandon has the shades and the patio door open. It's pleasing, to say the least. This might be the perfect Tennessee spring day.

"Right here, buddy," Brandon replies, standing.

He's been staying at my place while interviewing with real estate brokers in the area. His laptop is on the coffee table, surrounded by newspapers and glossy new home guides.

Happily, my friend is considering a move to Loveland, if he can find a professional group he jives with. He has a well-established real estate business in Atlanta, so it's a big deal to relocate at this point in his career. He's spent nearly a decade building key professional relationships. Like me, though, he's grown tired of the intensity of the big city. He is more than ready for a slower pace.

I grin from ear to ear. "You won't believe the afternoon I've had," I say. "I'm walking on air right now. Like, seriously. Do you see the fluffy clouds beneath my feet? I promise you, they're there." I point to my feet, having fun joking around.

"That good?" he asks, then he gives me a high five.

"Better. The best. The very best. Ever," I say.

I shove a hand through my hair. I'm rambling. I'm a rambling fool. I'm a fool for love, that's what I am. I'm not ashamed.

He laughs. "I see," he says. "Did this best ever afternoon have anything to do with Rosalie Flowers?"

"You betcha," I reply. "Who else?"

He high fives me again, and we hoot and holler like

college frat boys. It feels good. I hope we're not bothering anyone outside, since the patio door is wide open. Really, though, I don't care if we are. I'm in love with Rosie, and I want to shout it from the rooftops! I want the whole world to know.

There. I admitted it to myself. I'm in love with her. *I love her.*

"Do you have time for dinner?" Brandon asks. "You can tell me all about it."

"Absolutely," I say. "I'll run Maverick out to do his business real quick, then I'll change into my party clothes. As long as you don't mind me being over-dressed, I've got plenty of time to grab a bite to eat."

"Sounds like a plan," he agrees. "I'll take the pooch out while you change."

"You sure?"

"Oh, yeah," he says. "Mav and I have become pals. He didn't tell you?"

I laugh, then thank my friend for helping out with the dog.

I change clothes quickly, noticing that I'm not nearly as concerned about what I wear as I was this morning when I hoped I'd be seeing Rosie. I might see her tonight, after the party, but I'm sure I'll have time to come home and change first. She knows I have a work thing.

I sure wish she'd been able to come to the party with me. I'd love nothing more than to introduce—or reintroduce, technically—my Rosie to Dad and Jesse.

I can picture it now—me with my arm around

Rosie's delicate shoulders, a fancy drink in her hand while Dad and Jesse beam with pride because they can tell how happy she makes me. It would be a full-circle moment, given all the teasing and strife that happened when we were kids. It feels like, finally, all would be right in the world. Dad would still be frail, of course, but meeting my Rosie might give him much-needed hope for the future. I know he intends to live long enough to meet his grandkids one day.

Oh, well. I'll party without my girl tonight. She'll be reacquainted with my family soon enough. Like I told her, I'm not going anywhere. We have all the time in the world. Nothing could keep us apart.

"Ready?" I ask Brandon when I return to the living room.

He nods, then we both say our goodbyes to Maverick and head out into the warm evening air. Brandon rides with me, smiling as he climbs into the passenger seat of my Tesla.

Feeling happy this evening and with time to kill, I take the scenic route. We debate where to eat as we make our way over the winding road through Lieper's Fork. I always enjoy driving that way, passing through the little village and seeing the General Lee from the old *Dukes of Hazzard* TV show parked in the grass. Today, Barney Fife's cruiser from *The Andy Griffith Show* is parked there, too.

There are a couple of spots there where we could dine. Puckett's Grocery is always good. There's a new place called 1892 Restaurant that I hear is good as well.

"What sounds good?" Brandon asks as we roll slowly down the main drag.

Several guys with motorcycles wave as we pass where they sit parked near the Pot N' Kettle cottages. I give them a friendly honk of my horn.

"I can eat anything," I reply. "You're the guest in town. Why don't you pick?"

Brandon chuckles. "I certainly don't need anything fancy. Hell, even the hole-in-the-wall Thai place I saw in downtown Loveland works for me."

Immediately deciding to make my friend's Thai dreams come true, I step on the accelerator and head back toward downtown. "You've got it," I say.

When we arrive a short time later, we're seated by a lackadaisical waitress who doesn't seem thrilled to be there. Her name tag reads "Flo," and I can't help but crack a friendly joke.

"Do you go with the flow, Flo?" I ask.

She rolls her eyes as she tosses menus onto the table. "Never heard that one before."

I chuckle. "Touché."

We climb into opposite sides of a tall booth and tell her to give us whatever she recommends. She brings us two bottles of Lucky Buddha beer and two bowls of spicy Tom Yum Goong soup. For a hole-in-the-wall place where the staff is less than enthused, the food tastes great. I'm slurping down the last spoonful and wiping the corners of my mouth when Brandon finally gets around to the topic at hand.

"All right," he says, pushing his bowl toward the edge

of the table. "Tell me about your afternoon. I'm not sure I've seen you this happy since … well, ever. What good things happened?"

I lean back against the booth and close my eyes, endorphins still coursing through my body from my afternoon with Rosie. Now I know what all the fuss is about from people who are genuinely in love.

I thought I'd experienced love a few times before, but I hadn't. Nope. Everything else pales in comparison to this.

"Amazing doesn't begin to describe it," I say.

"I can tell," Brandon replies. "I thought you were waiting until tomorrow to see Rosalie?"

"I was, but I couldn't wait any longer. I decided today was close enough," I explain.

He nods.

"I appreciate your advice," I add, not wanting him to think I took it lightly. "Focusing on conversation and being around her without becoming intimate allowed me to reflect on our interactions. It gave me the chance to be sure of what I wanted. Sure that our connection was real. Sure that she was the woman I'd hoped and not just a romanticized version I'd made up to help myself feel better about the sins of my youth."

"That's serious, man," he replies. "Heavy, life-altering stuff."

I nod, then use a finger to trace the rim of my beer bottle as I contemplate my future.

"Today was the day?" Brandon asks. "Did you kiss her? Or what?"

I smirk. "Oh, I kissed her all right. And then some."

He leans his head back in raucous laughter. "Okay, I hear that. I won't ask you to go into the salacious details."

"Good," I say with a laugh. "I don't think Rosie would appreciate it, if I did. But um, yeah."

My shoulders rise and I inhale deeply as I think about it.

"How was it?" he asks.

Descriptive words flood my mind. All of the good ones. "Incredible, wonderful, amazing, beautiful, magnificent, awe-inspiring, sublime—"

"I get the picture, Merriam-Webster," he says. "It was good. Got it. I don't need every word in the thesaurus."

We laugh together, taking swigs of beer as Flo comes to clear our bowls from the table.

"Seriously, though," Brandon says. "I couldn't be any happier for you. You're a good dude, Patrick. You deserve nothing but the best."

"Thanks, bro," I reply, soaking in the compliment. "I think this is it for me."

He leans forward with both elbows on the table. "It?"

"My future. The love of my life. I realize I've only known her a few weeks … this time, as adults … but it's like we're meant to be together."

"Really?"

"Really," I reply. "I don't mean to sound all woo-woo, but it feels like it might be our destiny. You know what I'm sayin'? It started all those years ago. It might not have been all hearts and roses back then—"

He interrupts. "I believe the saying is 'all hearts and flowers,' which is actually kind of comical since you and your brother are Harts and Rosalie's last name is Flowers."

I laugh, running a hand over a shoulder. "I never thought about that. It's pretty awesome, actually. I'll have to tell Rosie sometime. You're slick, my friend."

Brandon waves the complement off. "Thinking out loud. Go on, though. I didn't mean to derail your train of thought."

"No worries," I reply. "You get the idea. I guess our friendship or whatever you want to call it when we were kids was the beginning of a trajectory that would lead us here. To today. To happily ever after, I hope."

We pause, letting the magnitude of my statement resonate.

"I haven't experienced anything like that myself," Brandon says after a moment, "but I believe in fate. I believe what you're saying is possible. Who am I to doubt it? I don't claim to know how things work in the infinite universe. I wouldn't dare try."

I place a hand on his forearm. "That's exactly how I feel. Whatever it is that happens for people when they find the *one*, I think it's happening for me. I just hope I can be the man she deserves. I still have a lot to make up for. You know?"

He nods. "I do, but remember what I said. The past is over. Move forward. Focus on the adult relationship you're building together now."

I get it. I nod firmly. "Yes. Exactly."

Before we can get any further into our discussion

of the meaning of life and everything, I catch a glimpse of someone familiar sitting at a booth on the other side of the restaurant, near the kitchen and restrooms. The booths in this place have such high backs that it's hard to tell much about the people sitting inside.

"Hey," I say, "is that Jesse?"

Brandon leans over into the aisle and looks. He has a better vantage point than I do. "Yeah, I think it is. Want to go say hi? We have to pay our bill at the front counter, anyway. We can swing by his table while we're up. Looks like he's dining alone."

"Yeah, of course," I say. "I have to drop you back at the condo before the party. We might as well get a move on. We'll say hey to Jesse on our way out."

In agreement, we stand and approach the table where my brother is sitting.

"Jesse, hey, man," I say as I reach out and give my brother a fist bump.

We get along fine and I consider us to be close, but we don't necessarily talk every day. Even though we see each other at the office most days, we stick to business there. Jesse doesn't know about my reunion with Rosie. I haven't had a chance to tell him.

"What's up?" he replies, smiling. He seems nervous, though. Something is off.

"Hey, Jesse," Brandon says. "Or should I call you JT? I know you go by that now."

My brother smiles slightly, but reigns it in. "Jesse is good for old friends."

"All right, then. Good to see you, man. Patrick has

been saying the three of us should hang out while I'm in town."

"Yeah," Jesse says, "good to see you as well."

"I might actually be here permanently before much longer," Brandon says. "I'm in talks with a few local brokers ..." He trails off when it's clear that Jesse isn't really listening.

My brother turns and glances toward the restrooms. It's then that I realize there are two menus on the table in front of him.

"Are you here with somebody?" I ask.

He makes eye contact briefly, then nods quickly. "She's in the bathroom."

Brandon and I look at each other and smile. "She, huh?" I ask.

"That's what I said," Jesse replies.

I'm tempted to tell him about Rosie right then and there. I'd love nothing more than to meet my brother's lady friend and tell him all about mine. I don't, though. He seems rattled and I have a party to get to. Instead, I take a breath, then say my goodbyes.

"Well, I hope the two of you have a nice dinner," I say. "I'll catch you later, at the party."

"See you then," Jesse replies.

"Bye for now," Brandon adds.

"Bye."

We don't get a glimpse of Jesse's girl. Brandon and I pay our bill at the counter, then we leave the restaurant and I drive him to my condo.

We don't say much on the ride home. The important

things have already been said. The silence is a comfortable one.

I invite my friend to join me at the firm get-together, but he declines because he has housing market research to do. The market in Loveland is booming. I can imagine it's a lot to weed through.

I wave as he gets out of my car, then I speed off into the evening. It's time to get this party started.

The car skids as Jesse steers it into the parking lot of the Thai place. He's going too fast. He'll lose control, if he isn't careful.

His movements are jerky. He doesn't have a smooth charisma like Patrick.

Come to think of it, he reminds me of *my* little brother. Adam Flowers is three years younger than me, so that makes him a year younger than Jesse. Maybe it's the age difference, but I'm getting major little-brother vibes right now.

Damn.

Seems like Jesse and I together would be like trying to fit a square peg into a round hole. And my hole is filled nicely, thank you very much. At least, it was this afternoon.

"We're here," he says unceremoniously as we slide to a stop and he puts the car in park.

"Good," I say.

Inside, the restaurant is quiet. Three tables are full,

but otherwise the place is empty. I'm disappointed because this means there's more pressure to make conversation. A loud, busy dining room would have been helpful.

A stoic woman points us towards a table and drops menus down.

With Patrick this afternoon, it felt like all the universe was conspiring to bring us together. If we had been in a Disney movie, birds would have been dressing me while forest animals built us a throne to sit on together—Loveland's own king and queen. Even Tim McGraw is a supporter of our pairing.

Now, I'm getting zero good vibes. It's not that I'm getting bad vibes, exactly. They're just … limp. Bland. Lacking.

I excuse myself and visit the restroom. I don't even need to go, really, but I take a few minutes to splash some cold water on my face and psych myself up for dinner. When I return to the table, Jesse looks … I don't know … irritated? Bored, already? Confused?

"So?" he asks as I sit down.

Is that even a question?

"Yeah?" I reply.

"You look nice," he says again. "Nice dress."

"Thanks."

"You work in the building with the coffee stand?"

Finally, we're getting somewhere.

"I do. You?"

"Not really. Or, not all the time …"

"I see," I offer.

The stoic woman returns with rolls of silverware

and water in red plastic cups. She mumbles something about coming back to take our order in a few minutes. We smile politely.

"I'm working on a project there," Jesse continues. "Remodeling."

Of course, he is. That makes sense. I assumed as much when I saw his bio on the Hart Design+Build website.

"Nice," I say, hoping I can get through this without telling him I know who he is.

The longer I don't say anything, the more awkward it will be when I do.

"It's good," he says.

"What do you do?" I ask.

It's a reasonable first-date question. Jesse seems like he wants to talk about himself. Maybe he will fill the airtime if I just ask him personal questions.

He leans forward, seeming more comfortable.

"I'm a construction manager. New builds and renovations. It pays the bills."

"Interesting," I say as I take a sip of my water.

He doesn't seem to realize that I'm one of the owners of the building. Well, technically, I'll be an official owner at the closing in a few weeks. At any rate, Jesse's assumption is noted. What do I look like I do?

I press on.

"Did you go to school for that?"

"I did. For a while. Then I took some time off. Then I finally got back around to it. My dad—I work with my dad. He wanted me to have a degree before he'd bring me on as a partner."

"Makes sense," I say.

Jesse plays with his straw rapper absentmindedly as he talks. He's fidgety. Rambling. I'm not. I'm completely calm and in control of myself. No baby deer legs in sight.

"I guess I'm behind the curve. But I'm getting there," he explains.

"Understood," I say.

He looks up at me briefly before turning his gaze elsewhere, mostly directing his attention towards the straw wrapper.

"What about you? What do you do?" Jesse asks.

Damn. Busted.

I bite my lip and look at the front door, thinking about how to respond and hoping someone will come in and save me before I have to.

"Um, I work at a flower shop," I answer honestly.

What other choice did I have?

"I see," he replies.

What the hell does that mean?

This conversation is clunky. I turn around in my seat and scan the room for our waitress. She's walking our way. Thank God.

Her name tag has FLO printed in big letters. She's Asian and doesn't seem to speak much English. I doubt Flo is her real name.

"What you want?" she asks flatly.

I order chicken and noodles. It's a safe bet. Jesse chooses something more elaborate that I've never heard of before. It sounds like it's his usual and that he's been here many times.

Flo scribbles our orders down on a notepad, then nods and takes our menus from us. She shuffles as she walks back to the kitchen.

Jesse and I look at each other. Neither of us wants to take the lead here. This date wouldn't be so bad if I hadn't just spent the best hours of my life with Patrick. The contrast is striking.

The rest of the dinner continues with more of the same.

Flo forgets my chicken and brings me plain noodles. I chuckle to myself as I think about my meat comment at Hemboldt's earlier. I suppose I've had my meat for today. I smile as I slurp down the noodles.

Jesse doesn't seem to notice. He doesn't seem to notice much. We aren't clicking, that's for sure.

The best thing about dinner is that I somehow make it through without divulging who I really am. I'm not sure how it happens, but it does.

I can't help but ponder the word flow and the name Flo as our waitress clears our plates. Patrick mentioning how things *flow* between the two of us makes me wonder if this apathetic lady fake-named Flo is a sign. Maybe it's a guidepost, urging me to remember the *flow* ... where I belong.

I don't blame Jesse for any of this. And I don't have bad feelings towards him. He's just a guy who asked me out and who happens to not be the right fit for me. If I hadn't reconnected with Patrick, maybe I'd be giving Jesse more of a chance right now. But in the end, it wouldn't have worked out no matter what. I know that. Jesse knows that.

And really, I'm not even mad at him for the hand he had in teasing me when we were kids. It wasn't about him. He was trying to look cool for his big brother. I get it.

Now, if I can just make it through the rest of the evening, I'll live happily ever after with Patrick and all will be well.

About that ... I had better find out where Jesse plans to take me. I assume he had more than dinner in mind.

"Where to next?" I ask as we pay the bill and head back to Jesse's car.

"Yeah," he replies.

Here we go with the brevity again. When Patrick says yeah, it feels like the single word contains volumes of meaning. When Jesse says it, it makes me want to smack him on the back of the head in the hopes that more words will spill out. The same way I feel about Adam sometimes. Little brothers. *Sheesh.*

"Did you have somewhere in mind?" I ask.

I suppose I can say enough words for the both of us. A few hours from now, this will all be over.

"Yeah," he says again.

"And?"

"There's a party I thought we might stop by, if that's okay with you."

"Sure!" I exclaim.

Having more people to talk to sounds great right about now. I'm dressed up. And besides, I don't think things can get much worse. So, a party it is.

I'm all for it. I'll socialize at this party and then be

done. Maybe I'll call Patrick afterwards to see if he wants to spend the night.

My body comes alive as I think about him.

Meow.

"Good," Jesse agrees.

"Good," I echo.

I'm not sure Jesse has said my name all night. I'm not sure he knows it.

CHAPTER 21

ROSALIE

The party looks lively when we arrive. It's on a rooftop terrace at one of the nicest hotels in town.

It seems like it ought to be cool on this spring night, but thanks to strategically spaced fire pits and patio heaters, it's comfortable. String lights are draped overhead, and a band is playing live music. A bar is set up on one end of the space, and a bartender is mixing drinks.

It's quite an upgrade from the Thai place. Jesse should have led with this.

"Wow," I say as we look around and take in the scene.

"Nice, huh?" Jesse says.

"Really nice," I say.

I relax a little and let myself smile. Maybe this won't be so bad after all.

"This way," Jesse says, grabbing my hand.

I hesitate. I don't pull my hand away, but I consider

it. I'm not sure I want to hold another man's hand now that I've held Patrick's.

I take a deep breath and tell myself to go along without making an issue out of it. Jesse is leading me to another part of the room. Nothing more.

Cool it, Rosalie. No need to overreact.

"Okay," I say, following him. "Where are we going?"

I have to raise my voice to be heard over the music. I don't mind though. The mood is festive.

"To get a drink," Jesse replies.

He leads the way, pulling me along behind him. He seems more comfortable here. He's more pleasant to be around, for sure, and we've only been here for five minutes. Maybe he's shy. Maybe the one-on-one was too much pressure for him.

"Okay," I say.

I scan the crowd to see if I know anyone. One woman looks vaguely familiar. I think I might have provided flowers for her wedding a few years back. If I remember right, her mom made most of the decisions. I didn't get much face time with the bride.

I smile sociably as Jesse pulls me past her.

I feel pretty tonight. It isn't exactly a conscious decision, but I shift into what I call glitz mode. It isn't quite as impressive as Beyonce's alter ego Sasha Fierce, but it's a little something like that. I pull my shoulders higher, stretch my legs further, and sashay as I walk. I know I'm attractive, and sometimes I like to be ogled. Patrick's attention has me feeling especially desirable tonight.

"What can I get you, Miss?" a male bartender asks as Jesse plants me in front of the bar.

At least he didn't call me ma'am.

But … it makes me miss Patrick a little. Everything Patrick says is charming. Including the word ma'am. This party would be even better if Patrick were here.

"Do you have anything flowery?" I ask.

I'm a sucker for all things seasonal. And a sucker for flowers, of course.

The bartender leans towards me to be heard over the Ed Sheeran cover of *Perfect* the band's playing. "How about a Cherry Blossom cocktail with gin, jasmine, and citrus?"

"Yes! Sounds pretty, and yummy," I reply.

He looks at Jesse. *Brent*, according to his name tag. No hidden meaning there … that I can think of.

"How about you?"

"I'll have a rum and Coke," Jesse says, still holding my hand.

"You got it," Brent confirms.

"Ah, a rum and Coke guy," I say to Jesse playfully. "A man who likes the basics."

He smiles at me, and I think he's finally warming up.

"I do what I can," he replies.

We both look at each other, smiling as Ed sings the word perfect over and over.

"I'm glad you're here with me tonight," Jesse whispers as he leans close to my ear.

No sparks fly when I feel his warm breath on my skin.

Oh, Patrick. I want you. Not Jesse. Not ... anyone else ... ever.

The setting is perfect, just like Ed says. I turn my head and gaze out over the twinkling lights of Loveland.

On any other day before this one, I would have loved this evening. I would have given Jesse the benefit of the doubt and time to get good and warmed up. He's not so bad. He's trying. He's definitely a nice guy. But he isn't *my* guy.

I pull my hand back.

Brent scoots our drinks across the bar, which gives me a good excuse to use my hand for something else.

Before I can taste my flowery mixed cocktail, a handsome man with deep brown skin places a hand on Jesse's shoulder.

"Jesse, my man," he says as he eyes me curiously. "I didn't know you were bringing a beautiful woman with you tonight."

"Dean! What's up, man?" Jesse exclaims.

They give each other a bro hug with firm pats on the back.

Jesse leans towards me again. "This is my friend Dean Shay. He's one of the architects at my dad's firm. We work together."

"Pleased to meet you, Dean," I say, shaking his hand.

"This is Rosa," Jesse explains. "She works at a flower shop in The Romantics building we're renovating."

Aw, hell, nah.

I was afraid of this. Lesson learned Ed: Never exchange names verbally when it's really loud unless you write that shit down. I thought Jesse was Jay. And he thinks my name is Rosa.

Dean is immediately puzzled.

"Rosalie's Flowers?" he asks. "They did my sister's wedding last year. But—"

Now Jesse looks puzzled. Maybe he hadn't heard of my flower shop before. Odd, since he's on the reno team for our building. But okay.

Another man comes up and stands beside Dean. An older man.

"Hello, Dean," he says. He quickly turns his attention to Jesse. "Son, who is your lady friend?"

I recognize this man from the website. And I remember him from my childhood. It's Richard Hart. Patrick and Jesse's dad. He looks older, and surprisingly frail. But it's him.

Dammit.

I open my eyes wide and try not to spill my drink as I work to absorb the shock.

This isn't just a party. This is the Hart Design+Build firm get-together that Patrick invited me to earlier. Which means …

My world tumbles into slow motion as I watch the inevitable train wreck happen around me.

"Rosa," Jesse says as he puts an arm over my shoulder. "Meet my dad, Richard."

"Hi," I mumble. "Hello, I mean. Pleased to meet you, sir. But this isn't—"

"Wait," Dean says, eyeing his mobile phone. He has my flower shop website pulled up with my face and bio enlarged. "I thought so," he continues.

"The pleasure is all mine," Richard says. "Any friend of Jesse's is a friend of mine. I'm glad to see my son with ... someone like you."

What is that supposed to mean?

Richard winks as he says it. He's already tipsy, ice clinking in the glass he's holding. He's slurring his words. And he isn't paying attention to what Dean is trying to say.

"Dude," Dean says, louder now. "Her name isn't Rosa."

"What are you talking about?" Jesse asks, his arm gripping me tighter.

I consider wriggling free and bolting, but it's all happening so fast.

"This is Rosalie Flowers," Dean continues. "*The* Rosalie who owns Rosalie's Flowers and who is part owner of The Romantics collaborative. She's essentially our boss. At least, she is on this project."

"Wait—" Jesse mumbles, his brow furrowed.

"It's right here. Look!" Dean instructs as he shoves the phone in Jesse's face.

"I knew a Rosalie Flowers when we were kids," Jesse muses. "It can't be—"

I open my mouth to explain, though I'm not sure what I'm going to say. The way this conversation is shaping up, it makes it sound like I'm some kind of fraud who tried to conceal her real identity. How ballsy of me. And how stupid.

Dean repeats my name a few more times: Rosalie Flowers. Rosalie Flowers. Rosalie Flowers!

I feel like Auntie Em should be here. Maybe I can

click my heels to get home.

The crowd parts and I look into it, scanning for an escape route.

And then, it happens.

He's here.

My Patrick.

He must have heard my name. He's standing, staring at me as the string lights twinkle on his handsome features. He's staring at Jesse's arm around me.

Patrick looks completely and totally heartbroken.

Oh, my God. This is horrible.

Tears spring to my eyes, and my drink drops with a loud crash as I raise a hand up to cover my mouth. The crowd gets quiet as they watch. The music stops.

Everything stops.

Patrick covers his mouth, too. Then his face balls up as fast as his fists. He looks like he wants to punch someone. Like he wants to punch his brother. Remembering the scene from the wedding last weekend makes me think he actually might.

"Patrick!" I shout, to the bewilderment of the other men around me.

Jesse gives me the strangest look.

But I couldn't care less.

How dumb I was to come here with Jesse. To be with Jesse at all.

What was I thinking?

Patrick shakes his head no. He's upset. It hurts me so badly to see.

I reach an arm out toward him, but he turns and

walks quickly away. Away from the party. And away from me.

"I have to go," I say, to no one in particular. "I'm sorry."

I chase after Patrick, into the lobby and down the stairs. I race as fast as I can. I have to catch up with him.

But he's gone. Disappeared into thin air.

"Patrick!" I call out, desperately. Repeatedly.

He doesn't answer.

I stand alone in the middle of Main Street. My world and my heart … are crushed.

CHAPTER 22

PATRICK

The Next Morning

"I'm going camping," I say to Brandon as I emerge from my bedroom with a bag already packed.

I'm wearing a Zac Brown Band t-shirt, shorts, and hiking boots, plus a blue BNA ball cap I once bought at the Nashville Airport when my bag got lost on a trip home for Thanksgiving. I probably look rough around the edges.

I don't care.

"Okay," Brandon replies.

He's eating bacon and eggs at my dining room table. The patio doors are wide open again and I can see that it's another beautiful day. It doesn't feel beautiful to me, though. After what Rosie—*Rosalie*—did to me last night, the whole world feels like a betrayal. The warm sunshine and spring flowers are nothing but a tease. Sure, they look nice and inviting, but they'll just wither and die, come fall. Why bother getting excited about them in the first place?

Yeah, I'm bitter.

"I'm sorry," I continue. "I know you aren't heading back to Atlanta until tomorrow afternoon, and I know we had plans. I don't think I'd be very good company. It's better if you spend the weekend without me. You'll have a better time that way. Promise."

"Are you ready to talk about what happened?" he asks.

"No," I say firmly.

That's not up for debate. I told him the basics last night. I'm in no mood to elaborate any time soon.

He nods slowly. "Okay. No problem. You go. I'll lock up when I leave."

I exhale, realizing I'd been stressed about Brandon's reaction. The fact that he's giving me the space I need only reinforces what a good friend he is.

"Thank you," I say, moving around the condo and collecting Maverick's things. I pack them into my bag along with water containers and food for us both.

"How long will you be away?" Brandon asks.

"A few days. Maybe more. I told Dad not to expect me at the office next week."

"Off grid?" he asks.

"Yeah, for now," I reply. "I'll see how it goes."

Brandon purses his lips, and I can tell he's worried about me.

"Don't worry," I say. "I'll be fine. We'll be fine." I look down at Maverick and give him a scratch under the chin. "I'm just really pissed. I can't deal with people. I need to clear my head."

"Okay," Brandon says. "Take care of yourself. Be smart out there."

"I will," I say.

"Call me when you come up for air."

I thank him again, then head out the door with my bag in one hand and my dog leashed at my side.

I'm anxious to get out into the woods, as if I won't be able to breathe normally again until I'm safely nestled amongst the leafy trees. Nature has always been a balm for my soul. I hope it will give me some measure of comfort now. My heart is completely shattered. I can practically feel the pieces hardening.

I stop to get my tent and a folding chair out of a storage closet downstairs. A neighbor sees me and I know she wants to chat, but I can't right now. I truly *can't*. I make an excuse about being late for something and blow past her.

I am late for something—my descent into the wilderness. It's either that, soon, or I fear the only descent I'll experience is into madness.

Maverick and I pile into my Tesla and speed away, slowing only long enough to roll the windows down on my way out of town.

"It's just you and me for a few days, boy," I say to my dog. "The weather's nice, and it should be good for camping. Sound okay?"

He whimpers, his version of talking back.

Maverick is a loyal companion. I'm grateful for his

presence, now more than ever. Even though I'm mad as hell at Rosalie and my brother, Mav accepts me. He'll stick around while I work through what I must. He'll wait until I find a way to put myself back together enough to face civilized society again. I'll get there. I'm just not sure how soon.

My phone rings, and Jesse's face shows up on the screen.

"Hell, no," I say, pushing the red button to decline the call. "In fact, I'm turning my phone off. I'm tempted to throw the thing out the window."

Maverick whimpers his agreement. Granted, he likes Jesse. I'm certain the pup will support cutting contact for the time being, though. At least, temporarily. I'll talk to my brother again … Someday. Today is not that day.

Mav puts one paw out the open passenger-seat window, then leans his chin down on it.

"Good boy," I say. "Get a whiff of the spring air. Let Mother Nature soothe your soul."

Now that the phone is silenced, I turn on some music. I fiddle around with radio stations for a moment, but decide to let 95.5 Nash Icon play. They often play old country songs. Alan Jackson's "Watermelon Crawl" is coming to an end. Hopefully, something equally upbeat will be next.

I round the turn to Highway 96 heading west when the new song begins. It hits me like a dagger in the heart. It's "The Dance" by Garth Brooks.

"Ouch," I say. "Right in the feels."

I let it play, and Garth's warm voice sings about being glad he didn't know the way it all would end. I agree with his sentiment that our lives are better left to chance. If we missed the pain, we would also miss the dance—the good, meaningful parts of life.

Put another way, I guess it's better to smile because it happened instead of cry because it's over. Easier said than done.

The song is one of Dad's favorites. When he and mom first split up and Jesse and I came back home to visit him, he played this song a lot. It's a remarkably zen way to look at divorce, I'll give him that.

I'm nowhere near ready to look back at my—what should I call it?—*relationship* with Rosalie and feel glad that it happened. It barely happened. It didn't even happen, really. It was a swing and a miss.

"I'm such a dumb fuck," I say out loud as Garth croons. Mav gives me a sympathetic look and a groan. "How could I have been so foolish?" I continue. "I thought what we had was something real. Clearly, she didn't feel the same way. How could I have been so wrong?"

I shake my head as I drive faster, the emotion threatening to overtake me.

"Am I cursed or something?" I ask. "I mean, am I destined to have relationship issues because I'm a child of divorce? Is that really all there is for me? Is it bad judgment? Bad luck? What?"

Mav groans again and shifts his weight. He's commiserating with me as best he knows how. Or maybe he wants me to shut up. I kind of want me to shut up.

"Fuck!" I yell as I punch the steering wheel. The horn blares and a nearby car honks back.

"Sorry," I say as I wave out the window.

The punch hurts my hand, which is still healing from the brush with those assholes at the Chestnut Hill Lodge last week.

Fuck me.

I turn the radio off and stay quiet for the rest of the drive.

It doesn't take long. Within twenty minutes, I reach the parking lot for my favorite camping spot along the Natchez Trace Parkway. There's a river nearby with a scenic campground on the ridge above. On a clear day, you can see all the way to Alabama. Dad used to take us here as kids. It's been a while, but I know my way around these woods. It immediately feels like a relief to be back.

Maverick and I unpack and settle in.

For four days and four nights, my dog and I hike, swim, and sit around, communing with the fish, the birds, and the forest creatures. The weather is nice. No rain, other than a few sprinkles on day two.

I don't even turn my phone on. I doubt I'd get a signal here, anyway. It's good to be off-grid.

I could stay this way.

I'm not sure I want to admit it yet, but as time goes on, my feelings toward Rosalie and Jesse *might* be starting to soften.

Might. Only might. It's a process.

Maybe Rosie and I simply weren't meant to be, as sad as that is. If she and Jesse can find happiness together, maybe I should let them. Maybe I should even support and encourage them. Jesse is my kid brother. I want the best for him.

It still stings, though. Rosie is—*was*—my girl.

Sigh.

On the morning of the fifth day, I'm kicked back in a hammock, eating a fruit and nut bar, when a fluffy bunny—of all things!—gets the best of Maverick. The creature makes a run across the ridge in front of us so close to my dog's nose that he's practically obligated to chase it. He is a hounddog, after all.

"Mav! Come back here!" I shout as I watch him bound toward a steep drop-off leading down to the river. "We can't go that way. Come back, boy!"

He doesn't turn back to acknowledge my concern. He just runs, full speed ahead, barking his head off as he goes.

"Maverick! Danger, boy! Danger!"

My heart rises to my throat as I envision my dog careening to his death off the side of the cliff. I haven't explored this particular section of the ridge to know exactly what he's facing, but I took a glance some fifty or so feet north while we were hiking the other day. I don't think Mav's odds of surviving are good, if he tumbles over the edge.

"Maverick!" I shout.

He's moving way too fast.

I break into a sprint, moving with all my might to catch up with him. My pulse pounds. I pump my arms and stretch my legs as far forward as I can with each stride. The sound of the river can be heard as we near the cliff. I'm overwhelmed with the realization that I don't think I can withstand another loss.

Rosie is gone. I can't lose Maverick. Especially after Dad's recent health scare. It's all too much.

"Maverick!" I yell, as loud as I possibly can. Tears sting at my eyes and my legs begin to feel like rubber. Like they might fail me. "Stop! Please, stop and come back here!"

He doesn't. The bunny goes over the edge. So does Maverick. I hear him yelp repeatedly as he falls. I reach the drop off point less than a minute later, my mind racing.

I hope he's okay. Dear God, please let him be okay. I love that kooky hound.

I take a deep breath as I glance over the side, bracing myself for the worst.

When the scene comes into view, I can't help but laugh. I let myself fall to the ground, landing on my ass and dangling my legs over the side. I look up into the trees as they sway in the gentle breeze, unconcerned with my drama.

Maverick's woofs at me reluctantly, as if he's humbly asking for my help.

He's fine. He tumbled into a stretch of thorny brush that, apparently, broke his fall. He's wedged in the brush, his collar snagged on a jagged branch. The bunny pauses nearby. Probably taking a moment to rub it in and bask in his freedom before scampering off.

"Maverick, you dog," I say with a laugh. "Literally. Ha! You had me worried, my friend. I don't know what I'd do without you."

I shake my head, tears coming for certain, now. They're a much-needed release.

I can't help but recognize the life metaphor here. Life, itself, is one big chase near a dangerous cliff, and you typically have no idea what fate awaits on the other side of the drop.

Sometimes, we tumble over the cliff, at the mercy of factors beyond our control. Sometimes, we become injured during the fall. We could even die. But sometimes, we land just right and something breaks our fall. Our job isn't to lament our misfortune, but rather to get up, untangle ourselves, and move the fuck on.

I'm reminded of one of Dad's favorite quotes by Havelock Ellis: "All the art of living lies in a fine mingling of letting go and holding on."

I've been holding on tightly for most of my life. Too tightly, I suppose. Isn't that what children from broken families do?

Okay, okay. I get it. I'm not saying I like it—and I'm still mad. But I get it.

I climb down and carefully extricate Maverick from the thorns, then we pack up and head home to Loveland.

CHAPTER 23

ROSALIE

A Week Later

I'm devastated.

It's been too many days since the party. And too many days since I've seen Patrick.

He isn't talking to me. He's ignoring my calls and texts.

I must have tried him dozens of times by now. I even went to his office. The receptionist said she had strict instructions to not let me in.

I'm home on my couch with Tabatha, just like when Jimmy broke up with me. Only this hurts so much worse.

I skipped out on work, leaving Rachael to handle our clients and represent Rosalie's Flowers by herself. It was shitty of me. But I couldn't bring myself to act like nothing was wrong. Especially with wedding projects. I would have been crying my eyes out, dampening the spirits of everyone involved.

I told Clara and Ella what happened … err, what I did.

They were mostly supportive, as usual, but they flat out told me I screwed up. Big time.

Ella gave me a good talkin' to in her gruff, mobster voice. Even Clara asked what the hell I was thinking. It was harsh coming from her.

They weren't hard on me like that after things ended with Jimmy.

I deserve every bit of it. I know. I just wish there was something I could say or do to make things right.

Jesse hasn't called. He's probably mad at me, too. I guess I owe him some kind of explanation. I'm just so heartsick about Patrick that I can't think about much else.

And so on.

I sort of wait for Ella and Clara to come back and make me get my shit together like they did after Jimmy. But they don't.

It's more than a week before there's a knock on my door from someone other than the pizza delivery boy. I'm in ice-cream stained pajamas with my hair in a messy bun when it happens.

"I don't want any," I yell from the couch, hoping whoever it is will go away.

"Rosalie?"

It's a man's voice. He's older than the pizza boy. But it isn't my Patrick.

Tabatha runs to the door eagerly. She wants me to be better. She probably wants to socialize with someone other than me.

"Come back another time," I shout. "Thank you."

Silence.

Then after a minute, "I'd like to talk to you. Can you let me in?"

Just go the f— away. I'm not in the mood.

"No," I yell out certainly, digging my heels in.

"Rosalie, it's Mike Taylor."

He says it quietly. Gently.

What the hell? What is he doing here?

"What do you want, Mr. Taylor?"

Mike is a friend and a colleague, in addition to Taylor's Florists being my shop's only competition in Loveland. I respect the man. We have a good working relationship. But I hate that he saw what he did the day Patrick gave me the corsage. It was an intimate moment.

Now, it's just embarrassing. Excruciatingly so.

"I told you. I want to talk."

I sigh as Tabatha looks at me expectantly.

"Okay, okay," I say as I get up and open the door. "But what you'll witness isn't pretty. I'm not ... doing well ..."

Mike smiles compassionately when he lays eyes on me.

"Can I come in?"

"Sure."

I wave him towards the farm table. I can barely look at it without crying. I haven't cleaned it since ... well, you know. Let's hope Mike doesn't want to eat on the thing.

We sit down and he clasps his hands together. He

seems wise. Fatherly. Maybe he'll say something that will help me forgive myself for ruining my own life … and Patrick's.

"I saw Patrick Hart yesterday," he blurts.

Wow, he's jumping right in, isn't he?

"So?" I ask, incredulous.

"Lunch time. At Hemboldt's. He was sitting alone at a table in the back. He looked pretty torn up."

Aww, Patrick was at our table.

I lean forward, interested now.

"What did he say?"

"That you broke his heart."

"But …" I say, tears rushing to my eyes. "I've been trying to call him. He won't respond to me."

"I had a hunch there had been some sort of misunderstanding," Mike explains. "Patrick said you were dating his brother and lying to him about it."

"No … I wouldn't … Not exactly …"

Mike nods.

"And I've spoken with Rachael several times this week. She's struggling to keep up with everything at the shop since you've been out. She's trying her best. I sent one of my employees over this morning to help her get caught up."

I sigh. Tears come fast and hard, rushing now.

"Mike, I'm sorry. I don't know what to say—"

He raises a hand in the air.

"No need."

I smile through my tears. What a mess.

"I don't know what to do," I plead. "Not a clue."

Mike leans his head back and looks at the ceiling as he collects his thoughts.

"Rosalie," he begins. "I saw you and Patrick together that day. And I've been around long enough to recognize true love when I see it. You two have something rare. Something special."

"I think so, too," I say, sobbing now. "We have a history. I hated Patrick. He teased me when we were kids, and I thought he hated me. But the day we stopped in your shop, he explained that he didn't know how to handle his feelings back then, which makes total sense. And I have … *strong feelings* … for him. Turns out, he's liked me all along. But I destroyed what we have. It's all my fault. Jesse—"

"Shh," Mike says as he places a comforting hand over mine. "Patrick told me about your history when he ordered your corsage."

"I want more than our history," I say. "I want a future with him. I can't imagine it any other way."

"Then don't give up so easily. *Fight* for him."

Interesting.

I glance over at a framed photo of my mama and me that sits on my kitchen counter. It was taken at dinner in Downtown Nashville on my twenty-first birthday. We're both wearing shimmery, off-the-shoulder tops for the occasion, and our long hair is styled much the same way. What would she say to me now?

Is giving up a recurring theme in my life?

Maybe not so much giving up as holding back. Being afraid to believe that I deserve too many good things.

Sometimes, I feel like I already have too much success, and I wonder how I could dare to wish for more.

Did being teased as a kid affect my self-confidence? Should I hold Patrick responsible for my insecurities?

Maybe I'm overthinking all of that.

At the heart of the matter, I suspect that I'm simply sad to move on with my life after losing my mama. It doesn't seem fair that I'm still here when she's not. But I *am* still here. I know she'd want me to move on. To find happiness. She'd be devastated to learn that I sabotaged a real chance at love. At having a family. At a bright future.

There, I admit it.

I sabotaged my budding relationship with Patrick. I should have canceled that date with Jesse. I should and could have done a million things differently. The realization hits me like a ton of bricks.

This is my doing all right, but it comes from a place of hurt, not malice. I wonder if I can ever make Patrick understand that much. I wonder if he'll ever be willing to give me another chance.

What we have is genuinely good. I want to fight for it.

"But *how* do I fight for him?" I beg Mike. "I've called and texted, and I've gone to his office. He has me completely cut off."

"Find another way," he says. "Where there's a will, there's a way."

He's right, of course. There's almost always a way. I knead my temples as I think.

How?

Mike smiles. "I'll leave you to figure that out. But *do* figure it out. It would be a shame to miss out on something as wonderful as you and Patrick have. I speak from experience. Barb and I have been married for thirty-two years. Every day with that woman is a gift. I can't imagine my life without her."

He stands up, and I leap to hug him. Dirty pajamas, be damned.

"Thank you, Mike. I mean it."

"You're welcome, Rosalie. Now go get him. Maybe take a shower first."

We laugh. Tabatha purrs approvingly as I close the door and lean on the back of it. I wipe my tears and strengthen my resolve.

Mike is correct. What Patrick and I have is special.

It's absolutely worth fighting for.

CHAPTER 24

ROSALIE

$\mathcal{I}$t takes another day to make the necessary arrangements, but I have a plan and I'll give it my best.

My plan starts with Jesse.

I can't pull this off without his help. I hope he'll talk to me.

I'm wearing clean clothes. And I've showered. Bonus, right?

Once I have everything in place, I pick up my mobile phone and dial Jesse's number. I hold my breath while it rings.

Finally, he picks up. I exhale.

But it isn't over yet. Jesse has to agree to both hear me out and assist with my grand plan.

"Jesse?"

"Yeah," he replies, predictably.

"It's Rosalie. Flowers…"

Silence.

"From The Romantics."

Silence.

"And … the Thai place and the party …"

"I know who you are," he snaps. "I do now, anyway."

"Right. About that. I owe you a huge apology."

"You sure do."

"I'm sorry," I say softly. "I truly am."

He sighs heavily. If he has a straw wrapper, he's probably fiddling with it right now.

I try again.

"I knew you didn't know who I really was. And that you had no idea about me and Patrick. It's complicated. But I should have told you everything when you picked me up that day."

"You think?"

"I do. I regret my choices. Believe me …" I explain.

Jesse sighs again.

"Look, I'm not sure I know the whole story, even now," he continues. "My brother is pissed off at me. He won't talk to me, and I don't understand why. He hasn't been to work. Apparently, he spent several days in the woods with his dog. All I know is that the two of you had a thing, but then you went out with me without mentioning it. It doesn't add up."

Now I sigh.

"I know," I reply. "I'll tell you everything and I hope we can be friends, but I need your help … with Patrick."

"You've got to be kidding."

"I'm not," I confirm. "Your brother and I have something special. He's the man I want to be with. The man I belong with …"

Jesse is silent for a moment.

"Are you still there?" I ask.

"Yeah. I guess I'm surprised."

"I know," I reply. "It surprised me too, which is why I acted like an ass, apparently. But it's true."

"Does he feel the same way?" Jesse asks.

"I think so."

I pause, then correct myself.

"No," I clarify. "I know so."

Jesse's quiet again. I can't tell what he's thinking. My fondness for him grows in the space of the silence, though. Maybe we truly can be friends.

"Then the two of you should be together," he agrees. "What can I do?"

I squeal like Clara and clap my hands.

"Thank you, Jesse! So much."

"You're welcome," he replies.

"Just think … " I offer. "If all goes well, I could be your sister-in-law someday soon."

"Too soon," Jesse says, chuckling. "How about you give me time to calm down before we talk about family dinners and in-law status?"

"I suppose I can do that," I say, smiling. "One day, we'll look back and laugh at our cringe-worthy dinner at the Thai place. What even was that?"

"Hey, now," he says, sounding warmer. "That was my favorite. I'll leave it up to you to help me find the right woman who likes it there as much as I do."

"Deal," I agree. "I know a few single ladies."

"Deal."

I think we've turned a corner. It feels good.

One down … and the most important one to go.

I proceed to tell Jesse exactly what I'm planning.

My surprise for Patrick will happen tonight at the very same hotel rooftop where the firm party took place. I've rented the entire terrace for a private party of two. I intend to explain myself to Patrick and ask for a re-do of that evening, so we can have the happy ending we deserve.

The same musicians from that night are ready to play Ellie Goulding's "How Long Will I Love You." Brent will tend the bar to mix us whatever we like. And Mike is making Patrick a boutonnière out of white roses and pink peonies, along with a fresh replica of my corsage.

Everything is set. I just need Jesse to get Patrick there, and then to keep him there long enough for me to say what I need to say. That's not an easy task given the fact that Patrick isn't speaking to Jesse, but I trust Jesse will find a way.

I thank Jesse again, then hang up the phone. I only have a few hours left to finish my prep.

I sure hope this works. If things go my way, I'll be in Patrick's arms by the end of the night. And I'll stay there every night after ... As long as stars are above.

For the rest of our lives.

CHAPTER 25

ROSALIE

The sun sets as I arrive at the hotel and make my way up to the rooftop terrace. Skies are clear, and the city lights sparkle against the evening colors.

I love Loveland. I can't help but believe I'm in the right place. At the right time. With the right people. I'm feeling optimistic. Taking action feels so much better than sitting around and feeling sorry for myself. No matter what happens tonight, at least I'll know I gave it my best shot.

I'm wearing red. I intend to make an impression.

My dress is a sexy off-the-shoulder number with a dramatic flounce sleeve. The body is fitted, and the hemline falls just below my knees. It hugs my curves and accentuates my … well, *blooms*. I've paired the dress with a smoky eye and red lips. My hair is styled in soft, sensual waves. I've accessorized with double-hoop gold earrings, bangle bracelets, and nude strappy heels.

I look good, if I do say so myself.

Patrick seems to enjoy seeing me dolled up like this. At least, he did at the Chestnut Hill Lodge wedding. When he lays eyes on me tonight, I want him to be speechless.

I hear the live music the moment I step off the elevator. The band is warming up with a medley of love songs, beginning with "Lover" by Taylor Swift. The sound travels throughout the space like a siren's call.

I hope it's enticing for Patrick when he gets here.

The string lights are up. They twinkle as flames in fire pits dance to the beat. Tonight, the staff has added tea lights in a row on top of the bar, along with rose petals scattered nearby. They've cleared the floor of everything except a cozy seating area near a large, roaring fireplace. The sound of the wood crackling adds to the ambiance.

It couldn't be any more perfect.

Brent is at the bar polishing glasses. The boutonniere and corsage are boxed neatly in front of him. He winks at me, then tips his head towards the flowers. The event coordinator for the hotel must have told him my story.

Err ... Our story. I'm determined that tonight will be an important part of *our* story. Mine and Patrick's.

I've been waiting all my life for this.

Like I said before, I'm a romantic. I believe in fate. I believe there's someone for everyone. And I believe in happily ever after.

I want my happily ever after, with Patrick. We were made for each other.

I'm nervous, but in a good way. A my-life-won't-ever-be-the-same-again way.

I don't have to wait long before I hear the elevator ding.

Here we go. This is it.

No one rides the elevator to this level unless they're coming out here on the rooftop, so I know it's him.

I hear his footsteps. One set of footsteps. He's alone.

I turn.

It's my Patrick. He's wearing dark trousers and a light sweater with three large black buttons down the front. The outfit shows off his muscular frame. His piercing blue eyes sparkle. He looks as handsome as ever.

My Superman.

Our eyes meet. He smiles. He can't help himself. He looks me up and down, and visibly softens.

Until he lowers his brows and forms his mouth into a frown. Now he's forcing himself to stay mad. To stay distant.

"What's this about?" he asks in a formal tone. "Jesse said we were having a business meeting with our dad. Am I in the wrong place?"

Right on cue, Jesse steps off the elevator. With a big grin on his face, he closes the glass doors to the terrace and locks them, locking us in.

"What the—?" Patrick begins.

"Enjoy!" Jesse says, then slow claps in our direction before heading back downstairs. "Don't worry. Brent has a key," he shouts just before the elevator doors close in front of him.

"Brent?" Patrick asks.

"The bartender," I reply, gesturing Brent's way.

"Oh."

Patrick's face goes slack. He doesn't want to be angry.

"Rosalie …"

"Quiet," I say. "Take my hand."

He does as instructed and lets me lead him to the middle of the terrace under the string lights.

"May I have this dance?" I ask.

As directed, the band begins *How Long Will I Love You,* massaging every note.

"Rosie," Patrick begins, and I melt when I hear him use my nickname. "We can't just pretend—"

I raise my finger to his lips and press gently.

"About that," I say. "It was a big misunderstanding. I didn't handle it well, and I owe you an apology. But it wasn't the way it looked."

"Really? You and Jesse left little to the imagination. He had a hold on you, and you weren't backing away. Come to find out, the two of you were on a date. How could you?"

"I know," I say. "I've wanted to explain it to you. I called. Texted. Stopped by your office."

"I can't fathom an explanation that would make things right," Patrick says sadly. "You aren't … who I thought you were."

I place my arms around his neck and pull him towards me.

"I'm exactly who you thought," I say. "*We* are exactly who you thought."

He wants to believe me, but he's skeptical.

I don't blame him.

"I'm a flawed woman with issues, like everyone else. I'm not perfect. I'm merely human. But I *am* who you thought I was. I promise."

"Then why?" he asks, pleading with his gorgeous blue eyes. "Tell me. Why would you go on a date with my brother after the day we'd had? After the feelings we'd felt? After we'd … made such tender love?"

I shake my head, then lean in close and press my cheek against his. He doesn't pull away.

"It's silly. I bumped into Jesse at the coffee stand in The Romantics building, and he sort of asked me out. With Ella's help, but that's beside the point. That was days before I reconnected with you. And I didn't even know he was Jesse Hart. It was loud when we met, and I thought he said his name was Jay. I said yes for the hell of it. We didn't have a real connection. It wasn't like—"

"Like our connection?" Patrick asks.

"Definitely not."

"Go on," he prompts.

"It just so happened that the date was set for the evening after you and I made love. It was as simple as me wanting to keep my word, so I went through with it. I shouldn't have, especially because I looked at your company's website and realized Jay was Jesse. It was a bad call."

"A very bad call. Dammit, Rosie."

"Agreed. But Patrick, Jesse and I were miserable together. We had a terrible dinner at the Thai place, and it was like pulling teeth to make conversation. It was worse than hanging out with my own little brother. There was never a spark between us. I spent most of the night thinking about you and wishing I was with you instead."

"But, you looked so cozy together at the party. Do you know how much it hurt me to see another man's hands on you? My *brother's?*"

"I'm sorry, baby," I say, pulling Patrick's head down onto my shoulder. "Jesse grabbed my hand to lead me to the bar. Then he put his arm around me when Dean and your dad showed up. That was it. You saw the absolute worst moment. A moment that wasn't an accurate representation of what was actually going on. I was looking for a way out when I saw you."

Patrick begins to soften more. He wraps his arms around me, and I feel a tear drop onto my shoulder. "There are things you don't know about, Rosie. My dad was sick. He's in remission now, thank God, but I worry—"

"I know. I heard, and I'm really sorry," I say. "My mom—"

"I know," he says. "Principal Livingston told me when I ran into her at Reggie's one day. I'm so sorry for your loss. There's a lot we need to talk about. A lot to share."

I wipe away a fat tear. "I agree," I say. "I rented the rooftop tonight for a do-over," I explain. "If you'll let me, I'll show you how that evening should have been."

He lifts his head and looks me in the eye.

"You did all this for me?"

"I did," I reply.

Hoping I'm not being presumptuous, I nod at Brent, who brings the boutonniere and corsage over.

"Patrick Hart," I say as I pin the flowers on his sweater, then place the corsage on my wrist. "I'll ask you again. May I have this dance?"

He pauses. It seems like the weight of the world rests in his decision. In a way, it does. I look at him openly, expectantly, wishing for him to see the love and sincerity I feel.

Then, finally, he nods his head, enthusiastically yes.

We hold each other close as we sway to the music. Patrick breaths in my scent as tears fill both of our eyes completely.

"So, no feelings between you and Jesse? At all."

"None. You can ask him yourself."

Patrick chuckles through his tears. "Yeah, I haven't been speaking to him any more than was necessary. I haven't exactly given him a chance to explain. Even though, I'm not sure he completely understands what happened himself."

I smile.

"There's time to sort it all out. The rest of our lives, to be precise," I say. "I've spoken with Jesse. He knows what you mean to me."

Patrick takes my face in his hands and nuzzles my nose.

"You'll have me ... for the rest of our lives? Even though I got mad without listening to reason? And even though I've been ignoring your messages? I feel like a buffoon now. A jealous, petty buffoon."

"Maybe you are, but only because I was a people-pleasing, immature fraud," I add with a laugh. "We're a fine pair, Mr. Hart. And yes, I'll have you for all the days of my life."

"Oh, Rosalie, my sweet," Patrick says, kissing me softly as he speaks. "I love you. I've loved you for as long as I can remember. I want nothing more than to be with you and to share a life together. I want us to be real. Not perfect, but *real*."

"I love you too, baby," I reply. "I want the same thing."

I smile so big my cheeks hurt as he continues.

"I want to kiss you every day. I want to hold you every night. I want to marry you. And to make babies with you. And to live in an old farmhouse with Maverick and Tabatha, and maybe some chickens."

"Chickens?" I ask, teasing. "Those might be deal breakers. I could be talked into a spotted puppy. As long as your buddy Tim McGraw will sing at our wedding. Oh, and I've been thinking we should get married on a rainy day, since it was raining when we met … err reunited."

"Yes, chickens, Tim, and a puppy!" he says. "Rain or shine! I want to watch movies with you. I want to eat hummus with you. I want to grow old and gray with you. And at the end of my life, I want to hold your hand, sure in the knowledge that every single day spent with you was a heaven on Earth."

"Don't forget that it will all be on TV, once Sonny and his crew are done filming," I add. "Won't that be something special to hold onto as the years go by?"

What exquisite bliss.

We do just that, living happily ever after.

THE END.

* * *

Get the next book in the series at
BrightHappyLove.com:

Down the Isle
The Romantics, Book 2

Happy reading!

STANDARDS OF STARLIGHT BOOKS
KELLY BRIGHT

Blissfully in love with her real life Prince Charming for a quarter century and counting, Kelly Bright knows a thing or two about happily ever after.

She believes love conquers all and that there's someone special out there for every single one of us. She writes emotional, feel good romantic comedy.

When her head isn't buried in a romantic book or movie, you'll likely find Kelly with Mr. Bright—scoping out charming settings for her next story or chatting up other meant-to-be couples and learning how they met.

Connect with Kelly at BrightHappyLove.com, and

on Instagram, Facebook, and TikTok at @brighthappylove.

www.ingramcontent.com/pod-product-compliance
Lightning Source LLC
Chambersburg PA
CBHW061552210726
48287CB00006B/2156